SILVER POCKET WATCH

The Shades of Murder

"Esther Valentine Chronicles"

A crime series of
Cold cases

Written by

Rebecca Conaty Bruce

DEDICATION

For many of my life experiences, I am grateful. It has made me what I am today. I dedicate this being my second series, and my first crime series... to those special friends who loved me unconditionally. My mother who always had a quote or life lesson ready to share with me or my children. Also, to my husband who encourages me daily. I always dreamed of being someone like Esther Valentine and now she has come to life in the written word.

Introduction

Esther Valentine tried hard to fit in, find her dream career, and put down the expected roots, but nothing seems to stick. She earned a black belt in karate, trained in the police academy, took college classes, became an amateur reporter, and still felt dissatisfied. Being a team player just wasn't her thing, solving crimes was.

Her next career choice came to her one day while helping a friend find a lost dog. Should she start her own detective agency and be her own boss? Her specialty...is solving cold cases. Esther charges a hefty fee to solve a cold case. When the police give up, the family hires Esther. Solving cases with even the smallest clue and the help of her long time friend Detective Mark Sailor, a member of the Texas Rangers Cold Case Unit. Esther commits herself to a case, then retreats to her sixty-five acre ranch in Texas to rest and re-group while awaiting her next case.

Prologue

A cold case is a crime, or suspected crime that has not yet been resolved. Esther Valentine uses even the smallest clue to solve cold cases. In Book 4, Esther is called to Austin, Texas to solve a murder. The clues have gone cold and the police have all but given up. Anthony Whitmore was found murdered at his lover's home leaving his wife and daughters devastated. Esther is hired to find clues and hunt down the killer. The family needs closure, Esther just needs a clue. Following the trail of events leads Esther to the rodeo where she has to go undercover to catch the killer. The only clue is a Silver Pocket Watch found at the scene. No one commits a crime without leaving something behind.

"No one commits a crime without leaving something behind"

"Don't do as the wicked do, and do not follow the path of evil doers"

Proverbs 4:14
New Living Translation Bible

"For evil people cannot sleep until they have done their evil deed for the day…. and have caused someone to stumble"

Proverbs 4:16
New Living Translation Bible

Chapter 1

Bullets don't lie and dead victims with their tongue cut-out cannot tell their version of the story. It is up to me to solve the case.

I am Esther Valentine and I solve cold cases. A crime that has yet to be solved. Families hire me to pick up where the police leave off. They never want to give up, they need closure. My mother named me after Esther in the bible because she was strong and Fearless. It is a hard image to live up to in my line of work.

After a case I go back to my secluded ranch south of Dallas, where I live with my little sister Marja, and sometimes my mother rumbles in with her thirty six foot RV to park until her next adventure takes her away. Marja has been trained well in weapons and computers. She is my knowledge expert. In my days we did not have computers, we had a library and the dewy decimal system. If I need information Marja can always find it. Even if she hacks the national police data base. Which we never speak about.

My cases come to me via my long time friend and current love interest Detective Mark Sailor. Detective Sailor works closely with the Texas Rangers cold case division. When a Family seeks closure after the case has run cold, feeling shattered over the loss of a loved one, Detective Sailor discreetly suggests a cold case private investigator. That is me. If the client can pay my fee, I will consider taking the case. I decide. I am my own boss.

My last cold case revealed the murderer as well as seventeen other missing persons that he had murdered and buried in his barn. I needed time to relax so I secluded myself at the ranch for the last few months learning how to cook. My new relaxing hobby. My ranch is sparsely furnished because the commitment to a permanent large hunk of furniture gives me anxiety. Detective Sailor and Marja are always giving me grief, even though I am getting better at it. I bought a couch while on hiatus. Five stores, three counties and a flip of a coin and we now have a couch to sit on. Still unsure if I love it or not.

It was a wet and windy afternoon with a noisy wind out of the North. Fall was leaving us and winter fast approaching. Detective Sailor called to tell me he had another case for me to look at. He agreed to come for a visit and try my latest food creation. Tonight it is Beef tips over noodles. Who knew making gravy was so hard. I have eaten most of my meals at diners while on a case. I love any kind of potatoes so this pasta was a real stretch for me.

It was dusk on the ranch when detective Sailor arrived and found me sitting on the back veranda watching a coyote family frolic while dodging tumbleweeds blowing in the wind.

"Esther, I brought you the file on a new case. It is a bit sensitive. The client insists on discretion. They wanted a good private detective for this one. Of course it has to be you"

"Discretion is my middle name Detective. What is the case about?"

"Anthony Whitmore was a married business man with two daughters. He was found murdered at his mistress' house. He was shot in the stomach and his tongue cut out. Police found very few clues and one set of finger prints"

"They did not want him to talk, but then they decided to shoot him? That is harsh. Sounds like "it is your word against a dead man game." Shaking my head. "The prints did not

match with anyone in the data base
Detective?"

"Not so far, it is as if he was
killed by a ghost. Someone under the
radar killed this man Esther"

"The mistress has been cleared I
suppose. Iron clad alibi?"

"Connie Munro, the mistress,
owner of the home had an alibi for the
time of the murder. She was picked up
by a friend, salon appointment then a
flight out of town for a girl's night out in
Vegas. It all checked out. She came
back and found the body near the pool
two days later. She has since moved
away, house is sitting empty"

"Where is the wife, Mrs.
Whitmore now detective?"

"The Whitmore home is in Round
Rock, Texas Esther. Just north of
Austin. Mr. Whitmore had a business in
Austin. Take I-35 through Waco, then
on to Round Rock. Can I tell Mrs.
Whitmore you will arrive in a few days?"

"Sounds good Detective, now let's eat. I cannot be expected to think on an empty stomach"

After a good meal, I thumbed through the police file the detective gave me then handed it over to Marja. She will look up addresses and do a search on people involved and search the police data base. I feel fulfilled having Marja around in ways I did not know was missing in my life.

After a late night talking with Detective Sailor I headed upstairs to clean my guns and prepare for the drive to Round Rock in the morning. I packed the usual three pairs of cargo pants and black pocket tees, knife, two guns, ammo and lip gloss. Routines are important. I hate chapped lips. However, this time I felt a twinge of rebellion and packed a pair of blue jeans and plaid shirt. If you are going to be knee deep in rodeo country then I may have to blend in.

In the morning I came down the stairs happy to have another cold case to work on after a few months off spending lazy days at the ranch. Lovely aromas were coming from the kitchen area. Rounding the corner I find Marja and detective Sailor dancing and singing in the middle of the kitchen using their spatulas as microphones… to sister sledge, *"we are family"* all while flipping pancakes and sausage. I have the best life. I grabbed a pair of tongs and started busting out some moves along with them. They stopped and stared at me as if I broke up the band.

"What?" I am all packed and ready to head to Round Rock this morning" Felling a little embarrassed. "Do you have my travel packet ready for me, Marja? I need to pull the trigger before the target moves; umm I must get on the road"

"What a buzz kill Esther, I think we were harmonizing well. Yes it is ready and I left it on the foyer table. It is nice to have a foyer table isn't it?"

I came by a foyer table on my last case. Marja was leaving my files on the floor by the door and hinted if we had a foyer table she would leave them there. I took the hint.

"Yes Marja I am glad you are pleased with another piece of furniture. I am working on getting more" It is not easy being committed to furniture. It is not like you can just buy a new piece if the old piece no longer looks pretty. "Do you need to brief me on anything before I go Marja?"

"Sure Esther, Round Rock, nineteen miles north of Austin, Texas. I found this interesting, grocery prices there are fourteen percent lower than the national average, there is an iconic water tower, and you can't miss it. Oh and I know you love the history so I found out that outlaw legend Sam Bass, the train robber, died in a gun battle with the Texas Rangers there in 1878"

"Really nice work Marja, but anything on the family I am meeting perhaps. Information that pertains to the cold case maybe?" I do love that Marja is a nerd for historical facts but she omits the obvious sometimes.

"Yes it is in the file Esther. April Bass Whitmore is the wife of the dead husband. Interestingly enough, her father is named Ephraim Bass. Don't know if there is a connection with the outlaw, still checking on that. The daughters are Summer Whitmore and Winter Whitmore. They had a whole season calendar thing going on I suppose, when naming their offspring. I also printed out the address to both the mistress house and the Whitmore home. That is about it"

"I will be in touch after I meet with the Whitmore family. Remember we are a team, a trio. No dance moves without me. Oh and book me a hotel in Austin, Marja. Don't forget you have two more driving lessons to attend"

"Already done Esther. Safe travels sister; I hope the new jeep runs good for you"

Detective Sailor walked me out to the new jeep I recently purchased. A shiny new red, four wheel drive hard top. After the last case I came home and gifted my old blue goose to Marja as a surprise and hired a professional driving instructor to teach her how to drive. I hope I do not regret giving up the old jeep.

After a warm kiss and hug, Detective Sailor loaded my back pack on the floor board in the passenger seat and I was on my way to Round Rock. He has been told to take another week off to unwind since the last case involved a new found serial killer. The accommodations from his department, pats on the back, letter from the city awarding him the key to the city, and the paperwork slap wore him out lucky man. He deserves it I suppose. I am not officially a private detective nor do I work for any agency although I have the training. I cannot attract too much attention from law enforcement, they do not like amateurs. I prefer to remain in the background, and Detective Sailor goes in front of the reporters and takes the gratitude for solving a cold case. It is our thing and it works. I just cannot see Esther Valentine, your friendly insurance sales person with a salary and retirement plan in my future.

Chapter 2

Arriving a few hours early to Round Rock I decided to drive around the city before heading to the Whitmore Home. The element of surprise is usually in my favor. The home is located not too far from the historic settler's park so driving around to see if there is any unusual activity before my expected arrival. I like to think clearly and get my head in the game before I approach a client.

I pulled up to the large brick home and parked in the middle of the circular drive. The lawn was perfectly manicured. Large trees were perfectly positioned on either side of the home providing much needed shade. Two white ceramic lions were posted at the end of the walkway up to the house. I rang the doorbell and backed up to the side of the door. After what seemed like a very long five minutes, I rang the door bell again. This time I heard movement on the other side of the door finally. A very cute teenage girl with super blonde hair and braces opened the door.

"Hello there, I am Esther Valentine. I am here to meet with your mother April Whitmore"

"I am Summer Whitmore, she is expecting you. Come on in. Mom is upstairs still fixing her hair. She is always late"

I followed Summer Whitmore through the foyer, down a short hallway and into a sitting room filled with bold log cabin furniture and cowhide cushions. Not at all what I expected from the outside look of the home. It was similar to a really fancy bunk house for cowboys. I took a quick look around the room then chose the cowhide loveseat. I placed my backpack on the floor in front of me as I noticed the bear rug that seemed to be staring at me. Teeth and all.

There were several deer and moose heads hung around the room as well as a large trophy case, several saddle displays and lasso's adorning the walls. Summer sat staring at me until her mother finally appeared in the door way. I stood up to greet her.

"You must be Esther Valentine, I am April Whitmore. I see you have met my daughter Summer, and her sister Winter is still in bed upstairs. Teenagers want to sleep their lives away I declare. Do sit down Miss Valentine and Summer here will get us a glass of ice tea" April said as she sat across from me.

The bear rug was between us and I swear its eyes were following my every move. Creepy rug. I waited for her daughter to leave the room before we began our talk.

"Mrs. Whitmore, I was told you would like to hire me to look into your late husband's murder. Is it okay if we talk freely in front of your children?"

"My daughters have been my rock and support. I only have my father left in my family and he lives with his young chirpy wife in Kansas. Summer is fifteen and winter is now eighteen. So I suppose it is okay for now. To start off I will send Summer out to feed our dogs then up to her room to finish her school work. Winter will most likely sleep through this whole interview"

Summer returned with a pitcher of ice tea and two glasses on a silver tray. She set it down on a side table near the loveseat then kissed her mother and left the room. Mrs. Whitmore poured our glasses and sat down before we started. She was a rather slim woman, smartly dressed with high cheek bones. Her skin was milky white and smooth as a porcelain doll.

"Mrs. Whitmore, your husband was found at Connie Munro's house several miles from here. That was two years ago and no new clues have surfaced. Did he have a restless need for some kind of action such as drug use? Were you aware he had a mistress?" I ask the hard questions first. It gets the sticky stuff out of the way. Like ripping off a band-aid.

"My goodness Esther, I heard you jump right in. I understand your question. Detective Sailor highly recommended you so I prepared myself. To answer your question I guess I suspected but ignored the signs. Southern women with a lot to lose often do that. I did not know Miss Munro prior to the murder" she said folding her hands in her lap. Many women ignore the signs of infidelity especially if they have no other means of income. It is a sad reality. "Where did you think your husband was at the time? When he did not show up at home for a few days. They estimate the body had laid there for three days when he was found. Did he travel for work?"

"My husband Anthony owned several western wear stores all over Texas. Whitmore Western Wear. He was an ex-rodeo, bull rider and had won several trophies and belt buckles. Until he was injured and doctors told him not to ride anymore or he would become paralyzed. He had an office in Austin. He would go to the office every day and on occasion he would stay overnight stating he had to take inventory, taxes, or paperwork. He had a team of employees so I suspected it was not true but I just said okay honey and let it slide" she sniffled. I have heard of wives pretending they do not see anything just to save the marriage. I know I would not be one of those wives. I can smell a secret from a mile away.

"I need to have full access to all offices, stores, and accounts if I am to take the case Mrs. Whitmore. I would also like to do a brief search of this house and grounds. Will that be possible?"

"Yes of course Esther, I am still a partner in the Whitmore Western Wear franchise. I will make sure you have full access. I need to know why he was taken from me and his daughters. They need closure" she sniffled then broke down into full ugly crying.

"Is there anything else about Mr. Whitmore's background you can tell me April? Any clubs he belonged to or business associates. Someone he was arguing with at work? I know this is difficult but I will try to get you the answers you and your daughters need"

"I apologize Esther; it is still hard to talk about. Anthony was a member in the Professional Rodeo Cowboys association until just before he was…brutally murdered. They were mostly a group of old rodeo cowboys. Friends. He wasn't on the board just a silent member now. I suppose you could look into that but the police checked out all Anthony's business connections. So I think"

"Did you two meet at the rodeo?"

"Yes I was the rodeo queen one year and Anthony asked me on a date. He was a tall and handsome rodeo cowboy. We were married six months later at the rodeo. When he was injured I thought our world was over but he started up the Western Wear Shop with a loan from my daddy" She said proudly.

"Sounds quite romantic Mrs. Whitmore. Did Detective Sailor explain my fee? I would like to get started as soon as possible"

Mrs. Whitmore brought my envelope of $5000 cash and walked me to the door. We agreed the second half would be expected if I solve the case. My brief tour of the Whitmore home was surprisingly uninteresting. The cowboy, cow hide theme continued through every room including an unexpected cow face toilet seat cover. There were wagon wheels carved into the staircase railings and a matching bear rug in the master bedroom.

I left the Whitmore home and drove directly to the mistress home on Harford street. It was located just on the other side of town from the Whitmore home. Mr. Anthony Whitmore was murdered less than five miles from the home he shared with his wife and daughters. What a shocking shame.

I parked in front and opened the file Marja gave me before leaving the ranch this morning. I was told by Detective Sailor the house was abandoned but to actually see it in need of repair was insulting to my senses. Vines had grown up the sides of the house as if mother nature was taking it back or trying to hide it from the world. A few windows in the front of the home were busted most likely from kids throwing rocks for fun. A shutter was hanging loose like a winking eyebrow. Gutters had small trees growing in them, the grass was tall, and I could see paint chipping. I am sure at one time it was a grand living breathing home. Now the front yard has become a meadow of weeds and wildflowers.

Marja had enclosed a copy of the deed to the property. The home was paid for, no mortgage. The property was listed in the name of Connie Munro and an anonymous partner. It is not currently on the market. Connie Munro could not be contacted for permission to search the house. I cross checked with the police report that described

Mr. Whitmore's body was found in the back of the house near the pool. He was fully clothed in blue jeans, western shirt, and alligator boots. No wallet, no identification, or money found on his person. Could have been a robbery gone badly. They took the money but not his expensive Cadillac parked out front. Police say it was towed. I wonder where that car is now?

I guess I am coming back tonight to search the house. I hope there are no spiders. I hate spiders. When I am on a case Detective sailor worries about me. He imagines scenarios of my dead body lying in some undisclosed location. Truth is I am more afraid of spiders than I am of being in a shoot out. I will probably die from a close encounter with a large spider. I can read the headlines now: *"Esther Valentine flailing her arms trying to get a spider off her shirt, tripped and fell into the deep canyon and broke her neck*"…or something just as gruesome. I will make sure I tuck my pants in my boots especially on night searches. I am usually pretty strong and tough but not with spiders. I can turn into a screaming little girl if one gets on my skin or clothing. We all have our faults I guess. I can take you down with a few karate moves, tackle you after a chase, or out shoot most men but crawly things are my weakness.

Chapter 3

I snapped a few pictures of the Munro house then decided to drive on to Austin and the Whitmore Western Wear headquarters. I placed a call to Marja at the ranch so she can do some digging into the Rodeo Cowboys Association and see if she can find a connection to Anthony Whitmore.

I pulled into the parking lot and chose a spot at the end of the building. Whitmore Western Wear was a fairly large building with wagon wheels adorning the front brown wooden walls. A balcony that would appear in most western movies was atop of the building complete with split rail fencing that formed a criss cross and saloon doors. Behind the western facade was an aluminum warehouse that stretched a full city block. Western Wear must be a hot ticket item in these parts.

Entering the front door I noticed a slight bell jingle to let the employees know someone entered. Soon a young employee wearing full riding gear including chaps was tipping his hat at me and asking what he can do to help me.

"I am looking for a nice cowboy hat as a gift for my boyfriend" I managed to squeak out. I am unsure if he likes cowboy hats. He has such a good head of hair; it would be a shame to hide it.

I felt it was best to appear as a customer first then try to ask questions about the dead boss. I may just buy a hat for Detective Sailor while I am here. The young salesman took me to the far side of the store where on display was rows and rows of choices. Boxes labeled Stetson, Outback, and Stampede were stacked almost to the ceiling.

"Let us start with what color you had in mind ma'am" the salesman asked.

"I think black, or maybe white with black trim. Is trim a real thing? I really don't know what color I want"

"How about the material? Do you want leather, cowhide, wool, suede?"

"Possibly suede, leather seems it would be too hot for the Texas heat"

"Well I am modeling a leather hat right now. Employees are required to wear the items we sell. I can find a few for you to look at then you decide ma'am"

"I feel like if you call me ma'am one more time we are not going to be friends. What is your name?"

"Everett ma'am...I mean Miss. I was named after a famous rodeo cowboy. One day I hope to be a bull rider. Do any of these hats look good to you?" He said holding two hats up for me to inspect.

I started trying on hats and looking in the mirror. I tilted them sideways and young Everett gave me a frown. He was serious about how to wear a hat properly and came in closer to adjust each hat. I did not know the size of hat to purchase for Detective Sailor so I chose a black suede Stetson and used Everett to model it.

"I think his head is about your size. He is a little taller than you but your head seems to be the right size. Can you gift wrap it for me?"

"I will see what I can do for you Miss. It will be our Whitmore Western Wear Christmas wrapping paper, if that is ok with you?"

"That sounds fine. Who is your boss, I would like to tell him how helpful you have been Everett?"

Everett paused, looked around, and then made a silly sad face stretching his lips into a frown. It was a little ridiculous and over dramatic. I stood there with a nonchalant expression waiting for Everett to either bust out laughing or burst in to flames for making fun of a dead man's situation. Even if it was his boss.

"Unfortunately he is no longer with us. He had a terrible...geez ...umm...some type of accident I guess you could call it that. He is dead. Gone for two years now"

"That is very sad to hear Everett, what happened to him?" I lowered my voice and took a step closer.

I wanted to give the appearance of secrecy. If someone thinks you will keep their secret they will give you all the dirt. If they perceive you are a gossip girl then they will step back and zip their lips tight. I learned quite a bit about body language being in this business. If they are right handed their eyes will look up and to the left if they are lying. The opposite is usually true as well. I extended my right hand to

him and he took it. I patted his hand
with my left. I wanted to appear
sympathetic. It worked. Everett leaned
in close and whispered.

"The boss, Anthony Whitmore
who this store is named after...well he
was murdered in cold blood"

"No....who did it?"

"They do not know yet but I
think it was his mistress. Everyone
knew Mr. Anthony had a girlfriend on
the side named Connie Munro"

"Did this Connie Munro work
here Everett?"

"Not officially, but she was here
all the time. Disgusting woman. She
wore way too much make-up if you ask
me. He was a married man with two
children. Mr. Whitmore was a skanky
man. I did not understand it all
because he has a beautiful wife"

"I really appreciate your time
Everett. I think I will be back to buy a
hat for me as well" He did not need to

know I have a nice hat already. Maybe Marja would like one.

Everett boxed up the hat and I left after paying. I will get Marja to check into the financial records of Whitmore Western Wear. I would like to know who is running the show now that Mr. Whitmore is dead. I am far from convinced Mrs. Whitmore was unaware of the mistress. It appears all his employees knew he was sneaking around. For now I will check into the hotel while I am here then head back to Round rock to search the mistress house. I will put in a call to Marja on the way. I learned my lesson. I need to keep Marja informed of my exact whereabouts. Hmmmm maybe I should be checking my new jeep for a tracker. Marja is very efficient.

"What do you have for me Marja?" I asked knowing she most likely already accomplished what I am about to ask her to do.

"The Rodeo Cowboy Association you asked me to look in to has a history that goes way back Esther. The group was created when a group of cowboys walked out of a rodeo to protest the actions of the promoter. He refused to add the entry fees to the total purse and that began a strike. Mr. Anthony was an early member because his father was a rodeo cowboy who was associated with the original strike. Another interesting tid bit Esther, there are newspaper articles from the time Mr. Anthony was hurt in the rodeo. He put all the blame on the rodeo clowns. The clowns went on strike. It was a big scandal"

"Interesting indeed Marja. Check into the bank accounts. Everyone at the Western Wear store knew about the mistress. See if she got her hands on any money, payments, or gifts. I am heading over to search the home now"

"Got it, oh and I still cannot find out who exactly the co-owner is on the Munro house but I have a sneaky suspicion it is Whitmore Western Wear. Be safe Esther"

At the hotel I tucked my pants into my socks and then into my boots. Threw on a long sleeve shirt, leather jacket, and hair up in my hat. I placed my small derringer in the lower pocket of my cargo pants and loaded my flashlight, extra ammo, and hunting knife in the back pack. No spiders getting in my clothes tonight.

It was a twenty minute drive from the hotel to the Munro house. I parked on the road just near the end of the property line away from the street light. I could get lucky and the front door will be unlocked. No chance. So I went to the side of the house and slipped my knife through the gate of the fence and lifted the bolt lock. Makes no sense to me. Lock and dead bolt the

front door but not the fence gate. I
closed the gate behind me. Luckily it
was a six foot wooden privacy fence so I
should be unnoticed. The grass was tall
and wet from dew already settling in.

I made my way carefully through
the grass encountering no snakes along
the way. I could see the pool and its
surrounding brick patio that reached
all the way to the back sliding doors.
Less grass to maintain. I shined my
mag light in the pool. The water level
was low and it had turned a lovely
green with algae. A few frogs jumped
when my light hit them letting me know
I was disturbing their home for the last
few years. The power is off and the pool
pump has not been maintained.

While the frogs sang I scanned
the entire pool area with my light. Then
I scanned the patio area near the
house. I can see a dark brown pattern
on the cement near the sliding doors. I
am sure this is where the Whitmore

body was found. No one even bothered to clean up the blood. It has seeped, dried, and stained the patio. I cannot blame miss Munro for wanting to move away after finding her lover dead on the veranda near the pool.

I jimmied the sliding doors and took the outside glass door off the track and set it aside. Shining the flashlight in the house and searching for spider webs before I entered. I stepped in with unbridled courage. A nasty rotting smell hit me. Musty but worse like rotten fruit. I decided to go left toward the kitchen. Nope. I do not open old refrigerators. Scary black mold and meat with maggots are not for me. I will skip that. I turned to go through the living area, den, and down a hall to three bedrooms. The first room had only a twin bed in it. The second room had a few more furniture items and a large vanity with a mirror. Marja would most likely ask me to bring that home for her. Nope, it is covered in three inches of dust and cat fur.

I felt the sneeze beginning and wrapped a bandana around my head to make a mask covering my nose and mouth. Cat fur and I do not get along. I moved to the end of the hall and entered what appeared to be the master bedroom. King bed, long dresser with a very ornate mirror and two wing-back chairs near the window. All the other rooms had curtains. These large picture windows in the master were bare. I stepped closer and noticed they had a nice view out to the pool area. I shined my light left into the doorway of the master bathroom. A very detailed spider web glistened in the light. This had to be a talented master spider to create such a masterpiece. I will respectfully decline to disturb it.

I turned back to the view from the windows and as I illuminated the pool area again, something caught my eye. A little glimmer of reflection. I scanned again trying to locate it. It has to be something very small and metal. I could not find it again so I decided my search of the bedroom was done. I do not want Mr. Spider to think I was a threat to his home or his beautiful web. Pretty sure I saw a late night fly snack tucked away in that intricate masterpiece. I can always come back for further snooping when Marja obtains the permission I need. I prefer searching abandoned homes in the daylight.

Chapter 4

I stepped back out of the sliding doors on to the pool patio and scanned the flashlight across the back yard hoping to see the item that sparkled earlier. I slowly circled around to the back of the pool shining my light in the overgrown azalea bushes. Just as I decided to take a step so I could see behind the bushes up to the wooden fence, a cat screeched meow! then jumped running over my foot to get away.

Jesus, Mary, and Joseph! My heart was pounding like a bass drum. I might have let out a tiny squeal and a little pee may have escaped. Allegedly. I am sure the cat was looking for a mouse to catch in the overgrown bushes but it sure startled me. I must have jumped four feet back. I put my hand on my revolver and took a few

deep breaths. I leaned over and put my
hands on my knees resting, catching
my breath. Darn cat!!

I shined the light searching for
the feline when I saw the glimmer
again. It was a slight reflection that
only caught with a certain aim of my
flashlight. Like metal when it catches
the light. I looked closer and I could see
it was coming from inside the skimmer
basket of the pool. With the water level
so low the flap keeping debris out was
in the open position. When water flows
it opens and closes allowing debris to
be caught but the flap keeps it from re-
entering the pool water. I circled
around the pool until it was right below
me then got on my knees. It was about
a foot and a half from the top of the
pool wall.

The frog choir was getting louder
with all the movement. I did not want to
reach blindly over the wall into the
skimmer. I just bet a little green visitor

has taken up residence in there so I will brace myself, but I had to see what was reflecting off my light. I backed up and found the cleanout cap embedded in the pool surround for easy access to clean out the debris. I unscrewed the five inch cap slowly. Waiting for something to jump out at me. It was corroded and hard to turn so I took out my knife and chipped away at it until it opened.

My intuition was right and two green slimy frogs jumped out as soon as I popped the cap. After I sufficiently shoo them away I shine the light in the opening. Seeing something I decide to use a stick instead of my hand. Not taking any chances. I think it is only frogs in there but it also could be a sneaky snake. Better to fetch a stick for the job.

Returning with my stick I scoop the basket handle and pull it out and lay it on the patio. Pushing aside the leaves and frog poop, I pick the item up and wipe off mud and grime to inspect it.

It is a pocket watch! An old timey pocket watch. The kind men keep in the breast pocket of a suit. I pull out an evidence bag and slipped it inside and sealed it. It was black with tarnish all but the stem at the very top. I was in luck that it reflected off my flashlight just enough to be found. I wonder how long it has been in this pool. At the time of the murder the pool was full. Maybe it went unnoticed or floated in the skimmer at a later time. I need to take it in the light and study it further.

I bid farewell to the frogs, the cat and the master bathroom spider artist and head to the side gate then back to my jeep. If I come back I will bring a can of tuna fish. I checked my boots for any hitchhikers, spiders, cats, or frogs before getting in. I hate spiders.

I turn the jeep back on the road to Austin and my hotel. I feel a good shower is needed. On the way I decide to go over in my head what I know so far. Mrs. Whitmore claims she never met the mistress Connie Munro yet all the employees from the company she partnered with her husband seemed to know about the woman who wore too much make-up. Mr. Anthony Whitmore was murdered apparently after his mistress left for salon treatments and a girl's weekend in Vegas. She returns three days later and finds him shot once and his tongue cut out.

"What could be a reason someone cuts out your tongue?" I wondered to myself. Mr. Whitmore might not have died from the single gunshot wound. It was the bleeding out and choking on his own blood that did him in according to the coroner report in the police file. What would be the motive? I definitely believe someone wanted to shut him up

or it was a message to the mistress perhaps.

I have to clean up this pocket watch and see why it was left behind at the scene. It is possible it belonged to the killer. No one commits a crime without leaving something behind. It is also true that the killer also takes away a souvenir in exchange. Note to self: must prop up on my pillows tonight and look over the police file again. With snacks preferably.

Pulling in to the hotel I park two doors down from my room and check the parking lot before entering. I put on the extra chain lock and push a chair under the door handle. I remove my revolver from the holster and lay it on the nightstand. Routines keep you safe. Changing your routine also keeps the bad guys guessing.

Stripping off my clothes I lay them on the floor looking for hitchhikers of any kind. Do not want a spider or bug of any kind left to haunt me later. I grab the pocket watch and head to the bathroom. In the bright neon lights I can see the pocket watch is old, possibly antique. It has a very ornate surface with a raised scroll design all over. It looks expensive. Someone will be missing this. Turning it over in my hand I can see no rust just a blackening of sorts so I am guessing it is made of silver. The lid-hinges appear to be in the nine o'clock position and it takes a little effort to loosen them. The stem and crown of the watch are at the three o'clock position. I push a few times and it finally opened like a clam shell revealing it's pearl. The watch may never work again without professional repair; there is water evidence under the crystal face. Inside the lid I notice engraving so I wiped it with some soft toilet tissue.

To my husband, Joseph West

Maybe it was a wedding gift? I will call Marja and she can do a search for Joseph West. He could be our murderer or just another visitor to the house of the Mistress Connie Munro. I am starting to feel itchy so I place the watch wrapped in tissue paper on the bedside table and head for a hot steamy shower.

Hotels are all different. I stay in a lot of hotels. The shower is what makes the difference. Yes I want a comfortable bed and clean linens but at the end of the day the shower can make a huge deciding factor. I want a big shower or a deep Jacuzzi bathtub. Marja did well on finding this place. The shower is all tile and big enough for two people. Hand held messaging shower head and glass shower doors. I am enjoying this tremendously.

Pillows fluffed, propping up, snacks taken out of the book bag and I have the police file in my lap. As I was munching down on a granola bar Marja called to check in with me.

"I found a silver pocket watch in the pool skimmer basket Marja. I will need you to try and find the owner, Joseph West"

"Was this at the Munro house Esther?" I knew she was asking because she had not obtained the permission for me yet. "Were you careful?" she asked.

"I was careful Marja; I went under cover of darkness. I just got back a short while ago. It needed to be done. I dislike searching in the dark because you cannot see all the critters that may be lurking. Like spiders...or scary cats that jump out"

"Cats?"

"Yes a cat Marja. Not to mention all the frogs that was living in that green slimy pool"

"I will look Joseph West up and text you the address if I find it before I go to bed. How do you like the hotel I picked for you Esther?”

“You did a good job Marja, have you heard from mother lately?” Mother was traveling in the north east in her RV. Rarely does she go too many days without checking in. “Hope she is coming back to Texas before it starts to snow”

“Mother should be rolling in any day now. She loved visiting Mount Rushmore. She says she brought us back a souvenir”

“I cannot wait to see what that is. Have a good night Marja and find me Joseph West”

Mother never brings back souvenirs, she calls them dust collectors. Maybe she is missing us. I will be interested to see what dust collector she has for me when I get back.

I skimmed over the police file, the coroner’s report, and statements from the officers that responded. No one apparently searched the pool. If the pocket watch belonged to the killer then the police need to step up their game. The statement from the officer on scene states the bushes were searched, house searched and a canine was brought in looking for drugs. Nothing was found. The Coroner stated that the bullet was from a snub nose .38 revolver. A common small gun, easy to conceal. The wound to Anthony Whitmore's lower abdomen, determined he was shot from about ten feet away. The bullet missed all vital organs. If he would have received medical attention he would have survived.

Someone wanted to shoot him out of anger, but did not want them to die instantly. Maybe they wanted information. When they got what they wanted from him, they silenced him by cutting out his tongue. The coroner suspects it was a buck knife, smooth blade.

Maybe the killer did not like the answers or was possibly afraid Anthony Whitmore would talk. Maybe Mr. Whitmore had already talked too much and needed to be silenced or taught a lesson. Or a little of both.

An awful way to end a life. Cannot scream out for help. Searching the coroner's report again I read there was a large bruising on the chest. So If Mr. Whitmore could have turned over and stopped the bleeding he still might have survived but someone stepped on his chest to hold him down so he would suffer and die.

I am dealing with a brutal cold hearted murderer that had a vendetta against Anthony Whitmore. Possibly a hit man.

Chapter 5

I fell asleep still propped up on the pillows. A stiff neck was not something I needed while on a case. Digging through the book bag I located the aspirin I keep in an emergency first-aid kit. Glancing down at the phone I noticed Marja texted me an address for Joseph West here in Austin. I checked my revolver and placed it in my waist holster, tucked the derringer in the pocket of the cargo pants, grabbed the book bag and headed out the door.

Having detective Sailor greet me with blueberry donuts was a luxury I am going to miss during this case. I hope his case doesn't last too long and he can meet me one day soon. Deciding to visit the Joseph West residence first then hopefully find a diner in town later. I love a good diner. I can survive without blueberry donuts.

The West home was located in the Travis Heights area off Lady Bird lane. I was pulling up to the front in little time from the hotel. The yard was unkempt and not mowed. Truck in the driveway had expired tags. I parked a slight ways down the road and walked back to the house and up to the front door. I looked around and noticed the windows had tin foil covering them. There aren't too many reasons a person covers their windows with foil to keep out the sun. Either they work night shift and cannot afford curtains or they have something growing inside they do not want the police to find.

Either one could be true so I banged on the door firmly and backed up to the edge of the stoop. I did not trust the sense of anticipation I was feeling. I put my hand closer to my revolver. In any given case I realize my hand is exactly eight inches from my gun. I was just about to do a second knock when the door opened.

"Are you Joseph West? I asked taking a step back keeping a safe distance.

"I am Joseph junior, and who are you knocking on my door?" He tried to appear tough and scary. He failed.

"I am Esther Valentine and I believe I found something that may belong to you" I replied. I instantly disliked him. His scruffy beard was holding on to a piece of last night's dinner.

"Well then hand it over Esther Valentine. That is a funny name by the way" he grinned. "Where is this something you have of mine?"

"Valentine is a family name. I had a great uncle John Valentine that fought in the Civil War. He was a hero"

I did not have to give him any explanation. You cannot choose your last name. "Do you own a pocket watch Joseph West?"

"Nah, you got the wrong guy lady" He snarled. He stepped back just inside, with his hand on the door ready to slam it in my face. I put a boot in the way and my hand on the door. It startled him just enough for the crumb to move in his beard.

"Since you stated you are a junior then is there a Joseph West senior I could talk to?"

"Look lady my dad died about two years ago" He stood up straight trying to puff his chest.

"So did your dad own a silver pocket watch perhaps junior?" His eyes brightened as he thought over the question.

"Oh yes, he did as a matter of fact. I stayed in the house after he left. I needed some money...ummm I was between jobs. So I took a watch to the pawn shop down the street. Lucky

Pawn Shop. I got some big cash for it, so basically the answer is still no lady. I do not have a watch"

We stood there sizing each other up. I was keeping one eye on that crumb that jiggled up and down when he talked. I could see past him into the dark room and smell the distinct smell of cannabis. He was no use to me so I took a step back. I never took the watch out of my cargo pants.

"Thank you for your time Joseph West Junior. I just want to say if you do not want to draw any attention to your inside farm then maybe you should mow the grass and buy some dang curtains instead of tin foil. It is a dead giveaway" I stared at his eyes as he turned to look back embarrassed that he was so clumsy allowing me to see past him.

"Are you with the police or something lady?"

"No worries junior, but you might want to look in a mirror. There is a little something just hanging out in that beard. I will be in touch if I need any further information from you" I replied and turned to walk away. As I started walking down the road to my jeep I stopped and looked back as Junior slammed the door.

I felt a kind of bleakness leaving Joseph junior. He is on the wrong path in life. My jaded outlook is that he will be in jail or dead in the next few years. I cannot save the world. The future cannot be predicted. I must move on and check out that Lucky Pawn shop. Maybe they can give me some answers that I can use.

Walking to the Pawn shop did cross my mind however; the new jeep is just as convenient. It is just around the corner. A few bicycles are displayed out front as well as a few lawn mowers. You know I am thinking Junior should have pawned this watch for a lawn mower. It is tempting to take one to his house and tell him to mow grass for extra money. You can always change a life with one act of kindness. Just not in the cards today.

I step into the Lucky Pawn shop as the burly man behind the counter seems quick to put something under the counter out of sight. Possibly a gun with the serial number scratched off. Pawn shops are not supposed to take guns but they get desperate for money and take a chance. The shop owner is a hefty man with a patch of black chest hair peeking out through the pearl snaps on his too tight plaid shirt. So I put on my best smile trying to get the best answers. It's the exchange method.

"I have a silver pocket watch I want you to look at for me" I asked. I knew if this was pawned here before he would recognize it immediately. "It is not for sale I want to know who purchased it before”

"I will look at it miss but records are private unless the police are involved”

"What if I was to ask you please? I really need to look at your records and neither one of us really want the police involved now do we?” I snickered as I turned my eyes down to the area I saw him place the item as I walked in. If I was correct he would catch my hint and pull out his books.

"I don't know what you are thinking but I am just not sure it would be worth my while to let you see the books miss” He snickered back.

I knew he was suggesting I slide him a few Benjamin's and he would open the books and walk away giving me a chance to find what I want without guilt. I do not carry wads of cash so I had to call his bluff. I pulled

the watch out of my cargo pants and
laid it on the counter.

"This is the pocket watch. It was
found at the scene of a brutal murder.
Now I could pass you a little cash...but
I am not going to do that sir. You are
going to look at this fine piece and then
tell me who purchased it. Afterwards I
will just simply walk out of your sweet
Pawn Shop and leave you to take care
of whatever it is you just hid under the
counter as I walked in. Look back in
your books, say around two years ago
maybe?"

We stood there sizing each other
up like two rowdy drinkers about to
fight in a small town pub. I stood up
straight and folded my arms across my
chest. Knowing full well the butt of my
gun pooches out just a little when the
shirt is pulled tight. He started to sweat
and his smile turned quickly into a
frown. One of his hands slowly slipped

behind the counter as if he was going to reach for a gun or a secret buzzer.

"Okay man" I said throwing my hands up in the air like I was giving up. "I can just call up Detective Sailor of the Texas Rangers and he will be here in five minutes. He is just around the corner at the suspect's house. Sorry I bothered you" I bluffed. He slowly became clear headed, wiped the sweat with the back of his big hairy hand, and put both hands back on the counter. I turned a little to the side and pulled out my mobile phone pretending to call.

"No...No...I got you. He conceded. "No need to call anyone. Let me just get the books and I will have that information for you in no time ma'am, you say about two years ago?" He asked nervously. "I do think I recognize this nice pocket watch after all. It was a cowboy or something I think he was wanting to impress a woman. Just hold

on I know just where to look" He said
as he went into the back room.

Sometimes a bluff works
smoothly and seamlessly. Sometimes
you have to bust a few heads with the
butt of your gun. He was gone only a
few minutes then came out with three
ledgers listing all sales. Pawn Shops are
required to keep records.

"Here it is ma'am, a Joseph West
Junior pawned the watch for cash, and
the very next day a young man named
Steven Andrew Miller according to this
record, bought it for one hundred
dollars. I remember him now. This is an
antique watch and I wondered what a
guy like him was wanting to do with it. I
thought it may be stolen or something.
He had on full face paint and a cowboy
hat."

"Do you have an address for
Steven Miller from his Identification?
He was required to show ID right?"

"Sure, sure I will write it down for you ma'am. Full name and address. I do remember this guy. He came in the shop in clown make-up and I thought he was here to rob the place"

"Was he a rodeo clown perhaps?" I asked. I never heard of the rodeo clowns wearing their face paint outside of the rodeo. "It is unusual isn't it?"

Sweat was rolling down his temples like a river. His hand was shaky as he wrote down the address for me. He glanced up, making no attempt to deny he was worried about a call to the police and handed me the paper.

"Yes it is unusual ma'am but I thought he must have come straight from the rodeo and did not have time to change maybe"

It makes me wonder what this pawn shop has to hide, but that cannot concern me. I stay focused on the case and let the bad guys get caught in due time by the police. Criminals and shady

pawn shop dealers always make a
mistake. I waved at him as I grabbed
the watch and walked toward the door.
Then stopped and turned back.

"I am new in town can you
recommend a good diner for me close
by maybe?"

"Yea, Nau's diner, it is the best"

"Thank you, I figured a man like
you would know the best place to eat.
Be careful with buying certain items
that could cause you problems. For
now, your secret is safe with me"

Chapter 6

By this time my stomach was doing flip flops. I should not go this long without eating. I located the diner and sat down at a booth in the corner facing the door. Ordering my usual eggs, bacon, and hash browns made me think of all the diners and café's Detective Sailor and I have visited. I should take the initiative and call him for once. He always checks up on me.

"Detective, I just wanted to check on you. How is your case going?"

"Esther, so glad to hear from you. I am usually the one doing the calling so this means you miss me right?" he snickered.

"Usually I am three days in to a cold case and you show up, so I am wondering if your baby blue cougar broke down detective?" I teased.

"Actually I just ordered hash browns at a new diner and thought about you"

"Esther, I wish I was there with you in that booth ordering hash browns. We are working on a case of four missing teenagers. They just pulled their car out of the river, four bodies inside. It is one of those cases. Very heart wrenching. How is your case going?"

"I am sorry to hear that detective. Sometimes the bad news comes in like giant wads of indigestible horror. Prayers to the families of course" It is never easy to lose someone you love to tragedy. It is also never easy to be the one who has to deliver the tragic news to the family. I felt the detective's sadness in his voice.

"My case however, is just puttering along. I found a pocket watch and traced it to the owner. Next stop is the rodeo in Austin to find a rodeo clown"

"That sounds exciting Esther, please be careful. They can be a rowdy bunch. I may be tied up here for a while. Order a double order of hash browns in my honor. I love you Esther"

That was the first time we ended a call with expression of love. A sign he is not himself. His case must be hard on his emotions. Whether you are involved in fighting fires, fighting crime, or solving cold cases, emotions are something you choke down until you can let them all out in private.

When the waitress brought my order I asked her about the local rodeo to see if I can get a feel of the layout. Like most, she was very chatty when it came to her town, the people, and her rodeo.

"I am from out of town and interested in visiting a rodeo; do you know how I can make that happen, miss?"

"Sure do hon; I am Kristy by the way. Austin is the home of the rodeo. We have a rodeo or activities for the rodeo, competitions and fairs all year long" she said getting excited. "What part do you like best?"

"I hear the rodeo clowns are something to see during bull riding competitions. They protect the riders and provide some entertainment as well so I assume. Are there any bull riding competitions going on around here?" My personal knowledge of the rodeo is only what I have read in newspapers while having coffee at the kitchen table. I had never actually been to a rodeo.

"Oh yes, I dated a rodeo clown once. They put on a happy face of paint but they are a rowdy bunch underneath that paint. They are like an exclusive boys club, members only. Almost like family, but closer if that is possible. Hard to get in, harder to date one. The times for the rodeo and competitions are listed in the newspaper. I will bring you a paper to the table as soon as I clear table five over there" she said as she bounced off to table five.

I have always said if you want the inner circle town gossip, just ask a waitress at the local diner. She knew one, married one, dated one, or killed one. Not always in that order. Everyone has a story to tell. Soon Kristy was back, newspaper in hand and even helped turn me to the page I wanted.

Austin Rodeo Association was having roping competitions, bronco riding, and a fair with cowboy mounted shooting competitions starting tomorrow. I am in luck, I thought to myself.

"The rodeo is quite fun hun, you should go. I thought about going because they are hiring extras to help with tickets, caring for horses and such. Waitressing is good but the extra money would help don't ya know"

"Thank you Kristy for the information you have been very helpful, I think I might just go tomorrow. May I keep the newspaper?"

I finished my hash browns and eggs, left a good tip for Kristy, and headed out to the jeep. My intentions are to drive near the location of the rodeo and come back early in the morning. I need to get a lay out of the land before I come tomorrow.

Driving outside the fence I can see a barn for horses, stands for the crowds, lots of hay bales and men in cowboy hats. A big sign was near the front gate that stated:

HELP WANTED, RIDERS, HORSE TRAINERS, BARN CLEANERS, AND TICKET TAKERS. JOIN THE RODEO. PART TIME AND FULL TIME
APPLY AT OFFICE

I rolled down the window and stared at the sign for a few minutes. I caught the smell of fresh hay and manure. The smell of the rodeo invading my nostrils was a sign I should not attempt to get a job here. I found little evidence so far for this case so my instincts are saying do it. I surely could not be a spectator tomorrow and expect to have a conversation with all the rodeo clowns. Good reason to ask for a job. Going over the pro's and con's in my head always helps.

However, if I was a part of the rodeo I would get a chance to blend in, have a chat, and slip in a casual interrogation without being suspicious. Detective Sailor would not approve. I shouldn't. Well maybe I could just check it out. I have ridden a horse before. My interest is peaked. I shouldn't. I could just check it out. *"What could go wrong?"* I ask myself.

I parked the jeep at the end of a row of cars near the employee parking lot and slipped my hat on; I always carry it with me, black leather jacket and pushed up my sleeves trying to look strong or something I suppose. I walk in the gate by the horse barns and a few people look at me. I wave and keep walking. I should at least check out what jobs are available. Too late to turn back now. I am standing in front of the office.

A rough hand grasps my shoulder. I reach up, grab the hand, and spin around ready to give someone a toss.

"Hey now, easy girly. Are you looking for someone?" said a tall older man with a nice looking goatee.

"Yes...I suppose. I am looking for the office. I came to see about getting hired on at the rodeo" I said nervously.

I do not want to come off as a weak flower but I do want everyone to know I cannot be pushed around. Tough is better than weak. The weak get picked on.

"Well you are a tough one. Bet you don't take any gruff off no one. I am Zak, the rodeo boss. I am the one you need to talk to, come on in the office here. I hope you can ride a horse"

"I can. Sorry about the arm twist. A woman can never be too careful these days"

I followed him in the office looking back to see if anyone saw. Sure enough I was drawing a crowd of a few men. I just whipped my hair around and followed Zak into the office. More like a shack really. I took a seat across from him as he sat behind a very old wooden desk. The walls were covered in rodeo flyers. It smelled like stale cigarettes and whiskey inside.

"What kind of job were you thinking about pretty lady?" asked Zak removing his hat and leaning back in his chair.

"I am not sure Zak. I am willing to do most anything I suppose. I need a little extra cash. I just purchased a nice vehicle and the payments are killer. By the way my jeep will be safe parked out there right?" I stammered as I was thinking in the moment. I did not have a real plan. This was an information gathering mission.

"Have you ever mucked out a stall before? Roped a calf or rode a bull Miss....I did not catch your name?"

"People just call me Valentine. You can just call me Valentine Zak. No I have ridden a horse in my younger days. I am not fond of mucking out stalls but if that is all you have I might consider it. I do like to dress up as a clown and I am not afraid of anything. Does that qualify for anything you have available Zak?"

"Well Valentine, I like you and I like that name. Most men around here working for the rodeo came from hard times. They like their privacy and usually go by a nickname. We pay in cash, no paperwork. It works for us and them. It is not illegal"

"I understand Zak. Sounds fair. I like being under the radar as well. So what can I do around here? Straighten the office, work in the kitchen, or sell popcorn?"

Hoping I can get hired on for a few days, poke my nose in the office, find Stephen Andrew Miller, and get out. The office did need a good cleaning and airing out so it sounded like a good suggestion.

"We do not have many females around here but I think you can take care of yourself. I need someone to ride a horse at the start of the rodeo and carry the American flag while they play the national anthem. Can you do that Valentine?"

"Of course, I would be honored Zak. Do I have to bring my own horse?"

"Nah we have plenty of horses Valentine. You can start with that tomorrow and if it works out I will slowly ease you into something else, if you follow the rules"

"I would be thankful for that opportunity. Before I say the final yes, what other things can you ease me into and just what are the rules Zak?"

"Oh you will learn anything you want Valentine. You want to ride a bull we can let you try that. If you want to work in the mess hall we can do that. As far as the rules they are simple. No hanky panky between employees or guest riders, no stealing, no fighting and never be late for the rodeo"

"I can live with that. Do you think I could try being a rodeo clown someday Zak?"

"It is a tight group Valentine, but maybe someday. I will see you in the morning at seven am. I will introduce you to the guys and show you around"

"I won't be late"

Chapter 7

I left the same way I came in walking near the horse stables. I am relieved Zak did not want me to clean out the horse stalls. I noticed a group of men starting to gather around a fire out behind the barns. They watched me as I walked by and I tipped my hat their way. This is a whole different world for me. I hope I can fit in.

Walking up to my shiny red jeep I worried if someone saw me they would think I had money and did not need a job at the local rodeo. No one seemed to be around so I climbed in and quickly left the area and headed straight for Whitmore Western Wear. I will need a few things if I am going to blend in at the rodeo.

I was in luck and Everett was working late today. When I told him I

had a job at the rodeo his mouth
dropped open.

"No way ma'am, how did you pull
that off. I am so jealous!"

"Simple Everett I walked in and
applied for any job they would give me.
You should do it too" I said giving him a
high five. I knew secretly Everett was
all talk. I could sense his fragile
personality would never apply for a job
in the rodeo. He was not the tough and
rowdy kind. He was best suited as a
Western wear Salesman. That is as
close to the rodeo he will ever come.

"I am going to ride a horse,
carrying a flag for the national anthem
Everett. Not the bull rider job I really
wanted but it is at the rodeo" I stated
giving him a smile and a nudge.

He caught on that I was joking
about the bull riding and let out a
maniacal laugh as abrupt and
meaningless as someone trying to hide

their inner fear. He quickly recovered and changed the subject.

"Okay we are burning daylight so let us see what we can get you so you look hot sitting up on that horse" he chuckled trying to hide the recent embarrassing moment.

I pretended not to notice of course and followed him to the blue jeans section. I brought one pair with me but they are not going to help me fit in. They are considered mom jeans I am sure. I tend to side with comfort over fashion. Everett had some great suggestions and very good taste in Western wear. We browsed through the fringed western shirts, jackets, and blue jeans.

A traditional western shirt is characterized by a yoke in a v-shape on the front and back trimmed with fringe, snap buttons, and long sleeves. Never wore anything like this before but I think I could get use to it fast. We picked out a white shirt with blue fringe trimming the yoke front and back as well as a white pair of blue jeans. I do want to look good carrying the flowing American flag tomorrow. Everett left me in the dressing room and when I emerged wearing the complete outfit, he gave me a whistle. I stood there admiring myself in the mirror. Everett then pulled a box out from behind his back and offered it to me.

It was a white Stetson hat. It was beautiful. Trying it on made me feel like I was living out a fantasy. OR a kid dressing up for Halloween...I bought the whole outfit and the hat. A matching hat for Marja was also in the works. I cannot go back to the ranch empty handed. In addition to the riding outfit I purchased two more pairs of blue jeans, new boots, and a few simple western shirts with pearl snap buttons. Everett tried to talk me into a bolero tie but that was just too much for me.

All set, Everett helped me carry my packages out to the jeep. I loaded the bags and boxes into the back seat and turned toward Everett.

"You may never be a bull rider Everett but I think you are a wonderful salesman with exquisite taste"

"*Stick to what you know and do it well* is what my mother always said. But if you dream of being a bull rider in your future, don't let anything stop you. Dreams are just ideas that have not come true...yet"

"I know I will never fit in as a bull rider Esther. I just wish I was brave enough to try it once" he said leaning in for a final hug good-bye.

With the lights going out in the store Everett turned to go in and lock up the shop. He stayed late helping me with my purchases and earned a good commission from it as well. I hope he gets to try bull riding one day. The closest he will come is a mechanical bull at a local honky tonk I am sure.

I pulled out of the parking lot and headed back to my hotel, parked two doors down and to the left and scanned the parking lot before entering with all my bags and boxes. I laid all the items out on the bed after locking the chain and pushing a chair under the door knob. Even a pleasurable shopping spree cannot make me forget my routine.

After setting my alarm for five am to ensure plenty of time to shower and dress I propped up on the pillows and got comfortable. Detective Sailor assured me he would call tonight and I knew he would over react when I tell him I am going under cover at the rodeo.

"What? Esther you cannot be serious. You are doing what?" Detective Sailor barked.

"Calm down detective I am not a frail little flower remember? I can take care of myself. I will be careful, diligent and in touch every chance I get. It is the only way to get in and find a way to talk to the rodeo clowns. I hear they are a tight group. You have to admit it is a brilliant idea"

"It is a brilliant idea but possibly dangerous Esther. We get calls to the rodeo for breaking up fights all the time. I will come down in a day or two, this case is winding up"

"There is no need for that Detective. If I am going to be under cover you cannot act like you know me. However, you can come to the rodeo and watch me ride; I will be the one wearing the cute outfit"

"Now you are just teasing me Esther. I will try to make it in time to see you ride in that cute outfit and I will bring you blueberry donuts. You cannot keep me away"

"I found a good little diner in town also. We can meet up there after the rodeo detective. Please don't read too much into this. I am on a case that is all. I need to see this through"

I hung up from talking to Detective Sailor and called Marja to let her know about my plan. I also need her to look into the rodeo financial records, the pawn shop and try to find the mysterious Steven Andrew Miller. I doubt I will get any sleep tonight. Riding in the rodeo is one of those items on a bucket list that most people put at the very bottom. Unless you were born and raised in Texas.

The alarm went off at five am and I rolled over to hit the snooze. I never do that. I am usually up ready to go. Worry kept me from getting that deep sleep I am used to getting. I thought about Zak and all the men I saw hanging out around the barns at the rodeo yesterday.

"Did I jump into something I shouldn't have?" I thought to myself. It was too late to back out now. I will see what happens today then make a decision if I want to continue. I am not even sure if this Steven Miller is a rodeo clown here. I just need to find a lead in the case. I still haven't figured out the motive for the murder. If I can find the owner of the silver pocket watch then I believe the clues will reveal themselves.

I pushed myself upright and headed to the shower. Glancing over at the outfit I laid out on the second bed I felt the flame of excitement come back. Deciding to be the best flag presenter I can be today. I am ready to rock this job.

Much needed pep talk done, I finished getting dressed, put on some lip gloss, grabbed the book bag and headed out the door. With my shirt tucked in it is harder to conceal my revolver so I chose to slip the derringer in my waist holster. Smaller weapon but at close range it can put a hurt on you and give me time to grab the hunting knife I keep strapped around the lower calf and tucked in my boot. Always be prepared for anything.

Butterflies in my stomach I pulled into the grassy area of the employee parking lot. There are not many cars actually because the regulars of the rodeo live on the grounds in the bunk house. My shiny red jeep sticks out like a sore thumb. I park it in between two old trucks and quickly get out walking toward the main gate. I see Zak and catch up to him. We never really discussed what I should wear. Maybe it was a test to see if I was serious enough to come.

"Valentine, you made it! I see you came dressed for the occasion. It looks good on you. I hope you brought a change of clothes because after you present the flag I am going to need you

to help out in the horse barns. We are
one man short. He got drunk in town
and proceeded to start a fight. Spent
the night in county jail" he said shaking
his head.

"I will help out where I can Zak. I
want to get to know everyone and
everything pertaining to the rodeo. I am
here to learn" I said following him.

"Valentine you run over to the
horse barn, the second one on the right
and get your horse saddled. If you need
help ask for Preacher or Tokyo, they
will help you. You are the opening act
so be ready"

Leaving Zak at the office, I
strolled over to the horse barn. I wanted
to run being so excited but I used
restraint. The big doors were open and
as I stepped inside I saw horse stalls on
either side all the way to the back
opening of the barn. It was as if the
horses sensed a new member of the
team was coming in and they all came

to the front of their stalls to greet me. Or perhaps they hoped I had a yummy carrot. Either way I walked slowly giving each one a nice scrub on the nose and forehead.

In the last stall, lying in the corner of the hay was a man sleeping. He popped his head up as I approached and I could see he was wearing clown makeup.

"Hello there lady, you must be our new flag carrier. Zak told us to expect you today. They call me preacher"

"How do you do preacher, I am supposed to find my horse and I was told you or Tokyo would assist me?"

"No problem, he is the second horse on the right as you come in. He is the gentlest ride. Stall number two. I will fetch your saddle and meet you there" He said spitting out a stem of hay he was chewing on. Note to self: watch where you step in the hay.

Chapter 8

I back tracked my steps and found the horse Preacher told me about in stall number two. The horse came right up to the stall door and greeted me. The name plate hanging on his stall was "Buddy." A beautiful brown color with blonde tail and mane.

Preacher was walking up carrying a saddle as another man entered the barn from the front. Strangely he also had on full clown make-up and a cowboy hat. He and Preacher were chatting about the saddle and the horse like I was not there so I turned to face them.

"Hi, they call me Valentine. I am carrying the American flag to open the rodeo today. And you are?" I said extending my hand to greet him. He grinned, looked down at my hand then reached up and tipped his hat. I

lowered my hand and smiled back.
"Wow, he just left me hanging there for a moment" I thought to myself. Maybe there is a *no touch* rule along with the other rules Zak told me about. Or I possibly found the first rodeo clown that hates germs.

"They call me Tokyo. This here is a Kentucky Mountain Saddle Horse named Buddy. He is old and gentle. Do you know how to ride or are you just a pretty face that Zak hired?"

"Wow Tokyo, yes I ride. So is it true what I heard? That the rodeo clowns are a tight unfriendly group. Tell me is it a men only club, or are women allowed to join?"

"Nah we like women, just not prissy women. We are all bull riders' first and rodeo clowns second, and that makes it exclusive. Your saddle is all set. Preacher and I go out with you at the start. You parade around and we fall back and entertain the crowd a bit.

Get the crowd ready for the good stuff.
Be nice to Buddy, it may be his last
rodeo" He said never cracking a smile
on that painted face.

Climbing up in the saddle was a
stretch for my shorter legs but I never
let on. Tokyo held Buddy's reins and
Preacher brought me the American flag.
I slipped it in the cup attached to the
saddle and sat up proud and ready to
ride. The three of us slowly walked to
the arena gate and waited for our
signal. I gave Buddy a nice pat on the
neck while we waited.

"You ride Buddy in a circle
around the arena, then stop in front of
the stands during the playing of the
National Anthem. We will do the rest.
After the song finishes you give a wave
to the crowd and ride back here
Valentine. You think you got that?" said
Preacher who was at my left side. I
looked down on him then glanced over
at Tokyo who was staring up at me.

"I got it. I got it. By the way, why do they call you preacher? Do you have a real name?" I asked.

"Because Valentine, if you are about to be gored by a large bull, you want to call the preacher. Now stop asking questions, we are about to start" He snarled.

Settling in the saddle ready to ride I wondered how I was going to find out which one is Steven Miller. How was I going to know if he is even here working at the rodeo without asking questions? They do not trust me enough to respect me. I must show them I am not just a bimbo Zak hired to look pretty carrying the flag.

Zak appeared in the middle of the arena. The stands were crowded and all began to cheer when Zak announced the start of the rodeo. He waved his arm toward us giving us the signal that it was time to enter the arena. I gave Buddy a slight nudge and he gently trotted out. I lead him with the reins to go right as we circled passing the stands. Everyone started to stand and men took off their hats and placed them over their heart. The National Anthem started blaring through the speakers as I made the final turn. Buddy knew just what to do as he came up the middle and to a stop facing the stands for the remainder of the song.

Afterwards the crowds clapped and cheered then some threw hats in the air. Zak announced my name and included Buddy the horse. I waved at the crowd as I pulled the reins to the right, gave another slight nudge and Buddy broke into a gallop as we headed for the barn. My few minutes of fame were over. It was quite a thrill I must admit. I stopped Buddy at the gate and turned him around as I watched Zak announce the clowns and bull riders. Several other clowns suddenly ran into the arena doing flips and acting silly. They joined Preacher and Tokyo in the middle of the arena. I counted five more, seven in all. When the announcer introduced them, all of them had nicknames. There was Trip, Baby Boy, Tear drop, Ringo, and Hippie.

I have my work cut out for me. Wanting to make friends with the ironically most unfriendly group of the rodeo will be quite a challenge. Marja has to come up with an old driver's license or something to help me identify Steven Andrew Miller or I have no clue how I am going to get close enough to find out. I don't know how this going undercover is going to play out when the odds are one woman against seven rodeo clowns. Not the best odds.

I stood there watching the rodeo clowns interact with the crowd. They are putting on an act. Yet, one of them is capable of murder. I guess the motive is what is confusing me. We do not know why Anthony Whitmore was murdered and we really do not know if the owner of the silver pocket watch is the one who did it. Mr. Whitmore's murder made such a small ripple in the world of murders. He was a rodeo cowboy, a business man and seemed to be well known. Yet Marja only found one article on the man and it was about his rodeo injury years back.

At this point I doubt my whole theory. Doubting my instincts. I have to remind myself of some facts. Steven Miller bought the pocket watch from a pawn shop in this town. He was a rodeo clown. The rodeo is in this town so I have to be on the right track. I will admit, it is a long shot. In the meantime, I am part of the rodeo. Rodeo clowns are usually also bullfighters or bull riders. They have each other's back so no one gets injured. Must be why they are such a tight lipped crew. It may also be the reason Mr. Whitmore was murdered. The article said he blamed the rodeo clowns for his injury. He spoke out against the boy's club. What a travesty.

I continued to watch the rodeo clowns until the announcer came back to the arena and announced there would be barrel riding this morning, a cowboy mounted shooting contest in the afternoon and bull riding this evening. This shooting contest peaks my interest. The rodeo clowns started running back to the barn where I was still sitting on Buddy the horse. They glanced up at me with some strange looks, never spoke, and jogged by me like I was an orange cone in the road they were trying to avoid hitting.

Steering Buddy around to head back into the barn I noticed the group talking. They stopped when I entered the barn and stared. I dismounted and took the reins leading Buddy back to his stall. I got an uneasy feeling. I was the new girl. Topic of discussion. Even if I was a man I was not in the club. The rodeo clown club.

Fiddling with the saddle, fighting off the urge to lecture the club of rodeo clowns about how rude it was to stare, Preacher entered the stall.

"Do you know how to get the saddle off Valentine?" He asked with a snarky attitude.

"It has been a while but I am sure I can figure it out. I am capable of handling any situation without any help. I noticed the whispering and staring. Are you going to introduce me to the rest of the group or am I off limits? I don't bite, I promise" I eased into the request hoping to not sound too soft or too tough.

"Those guys like to keep to themselves. You will meet them all in due time I am sure. Let me help you get this saddle off Buddy first"

"Are all of them also bull riders...do you do the bull riding preacher?" I asked hesitantly.

"Valentine if you want to get on with everyone here I suggest you don't ask too many questions"

"Excuse me for wanting to be friendly. I just want to watch the action and make friends. I also am very interested in the shooting competition. I am pretty good with a gun" I said waiting for a reaction. Maybe I also wanted to drop a hint in case they had any crazy thoughts that I was a push over, a tenderfoot.

"It is not like this with all rodeo clowns everywhere Valentine. This group has been through some tough times and we...well we formed a pact with each other. We watch out for each other. And some of us do not want to be seen without our clown make-up on"

"Even out in the town or at the grocery store? That sounds dedicated. It would irritate my skin"

"You get used to it. If you want to find out about the shooting competition just ask Ringo or Zak. Now take that brush and give Buddy some love before you leave the stall. Then make sure his water is filled. A good cowboy takes care of his horse Valentine"

"I am not a cowboy" I muttered helplessly. I am a cowgirl if I am anything. So much for fitting in. It is ridiculous to be surprised by anything people say or do these days. Preacher made it sound dang near impossible to get to know any of them. Don't know exactly what I expected to learn from that conversation with preacher. The one piece of information he did give was that not all the rodeo clowns wear their make-up all the time. So I will concentrate on the ones who are full clown, all the time.

Chapter 9

I do not have a picture of Steven Andrew Miller but I would bet my new boots that he is one that wears his clown make-up all the time to hide his identity. He most likely knows the police have not solved the murder, he would not want to be recognized.

I found Zak in his office and asked about the cowboy mounted shooting competition and he informed me that it was closed. The limit of competitors was reached.

"Maybe I can add your name to the list for the next competition Valentine. Have you ever shot a gun while riding a horse?" he chuckled.

I was immediately angry but hesitant to show it. I leaned on his desk with both hands and stared him in the eye before speaking.

"I can out shoot anybody you put
before me. I never miss a target"

"You are pretty sure of yourself
Valentine. You practice up and I will get
you in that competition one day. I
would love to see what you got" he
chuckled again. This time leaning back
in his chair. I could see his beer gut
jiggle. I stood up and crossed my arms.

"How about you tell me what I
need to do next or am I released for the
day Zak?"

"You don't want to get those
pretty clothes dirty so I guess I will see
you back in the morning. Bring a
change of clothes. Tomorrow is roping
and I will need an extra hand. You
might learn a thing or two. You just
might make a good rodeo employee with
that tough exterior. But no crying, I do
not allow crying round' here"

I was infuriated. I turned without
saying a word and left the office. The
guns were firing from the shooting

competition that already started. Thank goodness because no one could hear the angry words I was mumbling under my breath. There are plenty of female rodeo riders that can compete with the good old boys in this world. This makes me motivated to prove them all wrong. I am not a team player. This is why.

I walked back to the barn and said good bye to Buddy. I heard voices coming from the last stall in the barn so I got closer. I inched slowly and cautiously, brushing against the stalls until I was near the last stall. Suddenly I heard the hoof clops of someone riding in to the barn behind me so I had no choice but to stand up and walk straight to the opening of the last stall.

"Hi guys, they call me Valentine. I just wanted to introduce myself. Looks like I plan on being around working for the rodeo for a while. Might as well get to know everyone's name, am I right?"

They did not look pleased with me at all. The happy clown faces went sad rapidly. I felt foolish standing there. No one moved, they just looked at each other then back at me. "Are you going to leaving me hanging fellas?" I continued staring around the stall. There were four of them sitting with their backs on the wall, their legs outstretched. A cooler chest sat in the middle, beer cans in their hands. It was like a couple of boy scouts at a camping trip minus the beer. I shrugged my shoulders and look at each one. The horse rider I heard earlier came around the corner and stood behind me in the stall doorway. His voice startled me.

"You boys have no manners today? This here is Valentine, she is a female I know, but she is harmless. Now get your butts up and introduce yourself properly then get on out to the arena. The shooting competition is taking intermission because someone fell off their horse and needs to be checked out. Rodeo clown time! Preacher is out there alone!"

I turned to see who the booming voice was coming from. He had on no clown make-up but I felt sure it was Tokyo by the way he carried himself. He was very muscular. The sleeves on his shirt were tight on his bulging arms. One by one the men got up, dusted off their jeans, and filed out of the stall past me. As they passed me they tipped their hat and told me their names. No conversation, no how are you, nice to meet you just one word.

"Ringo"

"Hippie"

"Trip"

"Baby Boy"

I nodded at each one as they passed then turned toward the one without make-up.

"And you are Tokyo right?"

"Yes Ma'am"

"I thought I recognized you. So you took off your clown face?"

"I was competing in the mounted shooting competition. Came in second so far. I will be bull riding this evening. I only do the clown thing in the morning. Zak likes the crowd to see a group of clowns. I help out. I have been working with Zak for almost twenty years. Sorry about the guys Valentine"

"It is okay. I heard they are a tight knit group. I was just being friendly and it is easier to know someone's name than saying Hey You!" I paused looking for a reaction, but he gave none. "I need to go now but I will be back in the morning. They are not going to scare me away. No worries Tokyo"

As I walked away I had a feeling he was watching me walk so as I approached the second to last stall where Buddy is I turned back quickly to find out. Then walked on out of the barn to head to my jeep. Yep, I knew he was watching me.

I reached the jeep in the employee parking area and sat there letting it warm up. The afternoon sun is starting to go behind the clouds and the cool night will be here soon. You never know how Fall will be in Texas. We have had cool nights and cool mornings lately. I love the change in weather and seasons. Sure beats the heat.

As I am driving I try to make mental notes about who was who in the stall. Ringo was very tall, maybe six feet. Where Baby Boy was the shortest one. Possibly why he took the name of Baby Boy. Hippy and Trip were average size maybe five feet eight or so. All of them made eye contact except Hippy. Oddly, Hippy looked down at his boots as he passed me avoiding eye contact.

Tokyo does not follow the rule of wearing full clown make-up at all times and he has been with the rodeo the longest, and he is apparently the oldest. I need to write a few notes when I get back to the hotel. It never explained in the police report why Anthony Whitmore was targeted. It is listed as a random killing. I need a reason.

I pulled up to the hotel and parked two doors down from my room and sitting there I scanned the parking lot while I gathered my book bag from the floor board.

As I entered the hotel room and latched the second lock, pulled the chair to wedge under the door knob and turned on the lamp, my mobile phone rang. It was Detective Sailor.

"Esther how was your first day at the rodeo. Did you fall off your horse?" he laughed.

"Not funny detective. I have ridden a horse before. It went fine. I really enjoyed it. I am going back tomorrow and do it all again" I replied ignoring his laughing.

"Whoa Esther, why so touchy? I was only joking around. Are you okay?"

"Well let's see detective, I spent the morning living a dream of riding a horse in the rodeo. Afterwards, I encountered a chauvinist who doubted my shooting skills. Then the highlight was meeting the boys club of rodeo clowns. They do not like anyone infiltrating their boy's only clubhouse apparently. They gave me the cold shoulder. I did take a few notes but nothing that helps me solve the case I am working on" I said slipping out of my outfit and throwing my boots on the floor. "I am frustrated and my feet hurt"

"How much longer are you going to go with this plan Esther? I mean how are you going to find out if the murderer is among the rodeo clowns?"

"I don't know detective. Maybe I allowed my mind to conjure up this lead, but something feels right about it"

"I do not totally agree with your choice. Just don't get too involved with those rodeo clowns. I will wrap up this case later today and try to come see you tomorrow perhaps"

"I still need to be undercover detective. I can do this on my own"

I finished the call with Detective Sailor. I was not feeling good about our conversation so I put it out of my mind. What else could I do, he needs to trust me and I need to trust my instincts. There is something here I just know it, I can feel it. I plopped on the bed trying to clear my mind. *"Am I chasing something that does not exist?"* I thought to myself. I need to call Marja and go over my notes again. Detective Sailor put me in the wrong mood.

"Esther I am so glad you called, I have some good news. I was waiting to call you in case you were still at the rodeo"

"I just did a short ride this morning carried the flag and they sent me home. Anyway, I could sure use some good news right now Marja, what did you find for me?"

"I found Connie Munro, the girlfriend of Anthony Whitmore. She was skiddish but has agreed to talk to you by phone not in person. She was hesitant to give permission to search her house at first but I got her to agree. I can give you her number"

"Oh Marja that is wonderful. At least I can find out what kind of person Anthony Whitmore was before he was murdered. Send me the information and I will call her after I find food. Good work sis!"

"One last thing Esther, it seems your Steven Andrew Miller just doesn't exist on paper. I still have an active search going but this guy appears to be off the radar"

I cannot blame Marja, this guy is a ghost. I have heard about teens that drop out of school or run away and join the rodeo. They never get a driver's license or buy a car, or rent an apartment. They grow up in the streets, the circus, drug houses or in the rodeo. Nothing to show they even exist on paper.

"Go back all the way to high school if need be. He has to have something in his past on paper. Connie Munro may be the witness that unlocks this whole case Marja. I hope she will talk to me. Oh and can you check on Detective Sailor, he seems out of sorts. We kind of...well we disagreed on a few things...I may have hurt his feelings"

"He worries about you Esther and he misses you. It has been a while since you left for Austin. Stay safe sis!"

Enough talking on the phone for now. I need to find some food and settle in for the phone call to Connie Munro. I have not established a motive for the murder of Anthony Whitmore yet. I cannot be too hard on myself...the police apparently didn't either.

Mother always said *"every day is a new day Esther...*

The musings of my mother and mentor are what I rely upon in my moments of uncertainty.

Chapter 10

Walking into the diner I see Kristy the waitress and give her a wave. She smiles and directs me to sit in her section, which thank goodness was in the rear of the diner. I am still angry about my conversation with Detective Sailor earlier and really prefer to be left alone with my thoughts.

"Hey Hon, did you go to the rodeo yesterday?"

"Yes Kristy, not only did I go to the rodeo, I rode a horse and carried the American flag in the opening" I told her knowing it would bring on more conversation and explaining than I intended. Her face lit up like a mouse in a bucket full of cheese curds. "I was hired by the rodeo and I am going back in the morning to do it again"

"Get out! Really? That is so
fantastic. Just color me jealous. You
are living out a dream of mine hon, tell
me all about it" she said boldly taking a
seat across from me in the booth.

"It was nothing really. I enjoyed
it and the horse they gave me to ride
was named Buddy. I met the rodeo
clowns also. You are right they are a
strange tight lipped bunch" I
commented trying to change the
subject.

"Pffft…don't I know it! Listen you
be careful and stay away from those
rodeo clowns. I heard a rumor from a
friend of mine that her friend had a
boyfriend that was jealous over one of
them clowns and went to confront him.
Well rumor is the boyfriend up and
disappeared. Don't know if it is true but
after dating one I kind of believe it
could happen. Let me go and get your
order in hon. I will be back"

That is all I need is more rumors about the scary tough rodeo clowns. From what I gather, they cover for each other, have no manners, and do not let outsiders in their circle. I better prepare for a rough ride, if all the rumors were true of course. I mean who wouldn't believe a friend of a friend?

So there I sat, finally alone with just me and my food. My mind and my thoughts were coming together as I stuffed my mouth with perfectly cooked hash browns. I was anxious to get back to the hotel, settle back for a lengthy phone call with Connie Munro, and see if she can shed some light on why someone would want to murder her married boyfriend while she was on a girl's trip to Vegas. I do not know what to make of that. Girl leaves boyfriend for a fun trip with the girls and comes back to a dead man by the pool.

I left Kristy a hefty tip and paid the bill. Pushing open the door to the diner, a rodeo clown was coming in. He stepped to the side to let me pass and never made eye contact. He was the shorter one I met earlier so I assume it was the one they call Baby Boy. He never acknowledged that he knew me so I had to let it go. My instinct was to tell him how rude he was, but after all just because we were introduced does not make us friends. Can't read too much into it I suppose. I had no time to tangle with his manners or lack thereof I needed to make that phone call.

Heading back to the hotel I went over all the questions I would have for Connie Munro. I know the police questioned her, most likely at the station where it can be intimidating and make someone get their story confused. I need to approach this differently if I am to get anywhere with her.

Plan in place, pillows propped up and notebook in hand I dialed the number Marja gave me. It rang several times and I worried she got spooked and refused to answer. I tried again hoping she will answer and finally she did.

"Connie...Connie Munro? I am Esther Valentine. I believe you spoke to my sister Marja and she told you I would be calling tonight?"

"Yes Esther, I almost changed my mind and did not answer. I do not know what more I can tell you that I did not already tell the police two years ago"

"I completely understand Connie. I am looking into the case and I was hoping there might be some detail you can tell me that would give me a different perspective. I am sure the police were less than kind during their questioning"

"It was brutal Esther. I just came home from a fun filled weekend with my girlfriends to find my boyfriend dead. We just celebrated my friend Susan's birthday in Vegas. I was in shock. It still haunts me seeing him lying there," she sniffled. "Who would do that to him?"

"How about you start from the beginning Connie, take a deep breath. How did you meet Anthony Whitmore?"

"We met at his western store in Austin. He was kind to me when I came in to buy an outfit one day. I was going to ride in the rodeo there in Austin and I needed to look good. I rode and carried the flag for the National Anthem. It was a onetime thing. I was a fill in rider. They usually allow the rodeo queen to do it the week after the contest. It is once a year, usually they have a regular girl or someone from the riding club does it all the other times. I was not the rodeo queen but I filled in at the last minute because she was sick. The rodeo queen that year was a friend of mine. Anthony loaned me the hat I was to wear because I couldn't afford it for just one day of riding. It can be quite expensive. It was a white Stetson. Not on a waitress salary. I brought it back the next day to return it and Anthony told me to just keep it. We became fast friends, eventually started dating"

"When you started dating, were you aware he was married at the time?"

"I noticed the wedding ring but did not have the courage to ask about it right away. When I did ask about his marriage it did not matter, I was already deep in the soup I guess you could say. I just came out of a bad relationship so when Anthony Whitmore paid me attention I just ate it up. I was flattered" she paused.

Hoping to make her feel like she was talking to a friend and not a detective I let her talk. It was obvious that she still felt the pain even after two years. Mourning the death of a loved one has no time limit. There is no end date on the calendar of our emotions.

"Connie, I never had the opportunity to meet Mr. Whitmore. Can you tell me a little more about him? What was he like, did he like movies, did he love broccoli, riding horses? Just tell me in your own words what the man was like so I can get a feel of his personality"

In doing this I am hoping she will tell me any details that will lead to a motive for his murder. Putting her at ease did not mean anything really. I was not interested in what movies Anthony Whitmore liked actually. I did want to know if he made someone angry or if someone hated him enough to cut his tongue out.

"Esther, he was a kind man although he stood up for himself and did not take any crap from anyone. He could be stern and never backed down. If you were fair to him then he was generous with you. When I found out about his wife and family, I offered to end it, but he would not hear of it. I think his wife called one time and when I answered she said nothing. The caller ID said Whitmore. He really was an honorable man even though he was getting involved…umm having an affair"

"Sounds like he saw something special in you Connie. Was there Talk of marriage between you and Anthony Whitmore?"

"Truthfully I think it all started out of pity. He wanted to help me out. I had just tried to end a relationship with an abusive man when I met Anthony. My reward was a busted lip. Anthony saw that and decided to help me. He bought me the house so I would have a safe place to live. I was grateful"

So Mr. Whitmore basically saved Connie Munro from an abusive relationship. Some men try to save women like a father would a daughter. I settled back on the pillows and took some notes. Nothing is striking a chord yet. Anthony Whitmore sounds like a really nice guy. Maybe it was a random act of violence after all.

"Connie, may I ask who you were in a relationship before Anthony Whitmore, the one who was abusive?"

"I don't like to talk about him much. He was just someone I met at the rodeo in Austin. While I was still unpacking my things in the new house Anthony purchased for me, he showed up. He called me names and threatened me, said he would be back. It was my fault. I bragged that I had a new man in my life that was taking care of me in the way I should be. I told him the area and he searched until he found my car in the driveway. He was awful"

"That sounds like jealousy from an already unstable man. Did the two men ever meet up; did this man from the rodeo ever meet Anthony Whitmore?" I asked sitting up in the bed. If there was some jealousy going on this could be a reason to murder Anthony Whitmore in a fit of rage. It would definitely line up with a rodeo clown or another employee. I knew Connie was tiring of the conversation so I pressed just a little more.

"They did meet one time Esther and got into a huge yelling match. I think they recognized each other from Anthony's old rodeo days or something. It ended with Anthony slamming the door in his face. I never saw him again. I left the next day for my trip to Vegas. I told the police about it"

"Connie one more question. Do you know a Steven Andrew Miller?"

"No, not that I can remember"

"How about a Joseph West Junior or Senior?"

"No, why?"

"Can you at least tell me the name of your ex boyfriend that worked at the rodeo Connie?"

"Esther, I am still afraid of him. That is why I left and I am in hiding. If you talk to him, he will come looking for me! I told the police, it is in the report I am sure. He went by a nickname. He never told me his real name anyway!" she blasted through the phone.

"I understand Connie, but can you tell me what he did in the rodeo?"

"He was umm…a rodeo clown, but that is all I am going to say. I hope you understand. I don't want any trouble from him"

She hung up the phone before I could ask her about the Silver Pocket Watch. Perhaps I won't need to if I can find a way to discover the ex's identity another way.

Chapter 11

Pondering all the information Connie Munro, the mistress told me as I always do analyze afterwards. Details learned so far. If the ex-boyfriend was jealous that could be a motive. I scoured the police file and I do not recall any name or nickname of a rodeo clown mentioned. I should not play the scenarios over in my mind but I could not help it. I usually go with my gut feelings, my instincts. My gut feeling was telling me the murderer was a rodeo clown, who purchased a Silver pocket watch from a pawn shop, and killed Anthony Whitmore in a fit of jealous rage. I closed up my notes and began cleaning my revolver. Cleaning my guns is relaxing and maintenance is important too.

Following my instincts is also important when it comes to safety. My instincts are telling me I should tuck my revolver in my waist holster in the morning when I return to the rodeo and not my derringer!

I did not come here to change careers and join the rodeo. I am here to solve a murder and I may have to push those rodeo clowns for some answers. Rodeo clowns are supposed to bring joy to the crowd. Me pushing my nose in their business may not be a joyful situation. I am going in prepared.

As I contemplated a plan to get the rodeo clowns to talk, I realized the last time I talked to Detective Sailor we did not end it on a good note. Marja is right, he cannot help but to worry about me. I will give him a quick call before I go to sleep.

"Hello Esther, you are up late, is everything going alright? I did not expect to hear from you seeing that you are under cover and all..."

"Very funny detective. I told you I would be diligent and keep in touch. I am keeping my word which should put you at ease"

"So you only called me to put me at ease Esther?"

"Why are you being difficult detective? This is what I do for a living. I am doing what I love, so do not make me choose between you and the job. It is not fair. I think I might have had a break in the case, or at least a gut feeling of what could have happened. Can't you be happy for me?"

"Esther I support you in your efforts, heck I am the one that finds the jobs for you. If I feel you are not safe it makes me regret my decision of ever giving you the lead"

"I want it all detective. I want the man I love and I want to solve cold cases. Cut me some slack. I need to ask you something that pertains to my case, if that is okay with you?”

"Ask away Esther. I am sorry if I do not seem supportive. I am…I do support you. I wish I was there. Wait…are you saying I am the man you love Esther?"

"Don't get cheeky Detective Sailor. When I questioned Connie Munro she stated that she told the police the nickname of her ex-boyfriend who was a rodeo clown. However I have scoured the file and I do not see it anywhere. Was it accidentally omitted from the officer's notes?"

"That does seem strange. We spend hours on paperwork. I will dig around a little and see if I can find out something. She would not tell you his name?"

"No she said he was abusive and she was afraid. It made sense I suppose, I can understand her reasons. I dread telling you this detective, but I am thinking I might need to stir up the rodeo clowns a little. Maybe push for information and see if someone snaps. It is a tactic that usually brings results. Do not worry about me. I was trained well, by the best. And I will be packing my revolver tomorrow. I will call you after the morning show"

"Thanks Esther, now I won't sleep till I hear from you again. Be safe. I miss your face"

Hanging up the phone with Detective Sailor, I could sense the inner turmoil that was going on in him. On one hand he is the one who mentored me in the police academy; he knows I am well trained to take care of myself. On the other hand he worries because he loves me and the fact that I am a woman. That last part bothers me the most. I imagine it is better to be loved and missed than not be loved at all. I need to sleep so I can be at the rodeo early to carry the flag during the national anthem.

The next morning I arrive early and head to the barn after hiding my jeep between the barn and an old truck. I backed in to give me a clean fast retreat, if needed. Entering the barn I stopped at Buddy the horse to give him a nice head scratch. Buddy nudged me when I stopped always wanting more. He leaned forward and put his head on my shoulder. *"I wonder if horses can get depressed and lonely,"* I thought to myself. Living in a small stall most of your life has to have some kind of effect on them. Horses are meant to run in a pasture, free and wild kicking up their heels. The life of a rodeo horse, not always good.

After some generous loving and scratching time I moved quietly down the barn past the other stalls hoping to find a few rodeo clowns hanging out in the last stall like before. To my surprise there was only one. Sleeping in the hay with a blanket covering his entire body. The only item sticking out was his boots. Without thinking, I knocked on the stall wall. In a flash he jumped up throwing off the blanket and aimed a gun at me. I backed up and placed my hand on the butt of my revolver.

"Valentine! You should never sneak up on someone like that!" he said lowering the weapon.

It was too late. I saw the gun. I took a step in to the stall prepared to diffuse the situation. It was the rodeo clown they call Trip I believe. He ruffled his hair thinking about his next words.

"You are the one they call Trip right?" Why do you sleep with a gun?"

"One of us always sleeps in the barn to watch the horses. You should not be in here so early, you startled me Valentine. You should be more careful!"

"I did knock"

"Why are you here Valentine? I should probably go wake up Tokyo, he is going to be furious"

"No, it is no biggie really. It is not necessary. Let him sleep. I was just wondering if you knew where I could get a hot cup of coffee" Thinking fast on my feet as they say. I need a good distraction. "I saw nothing, just put the gun away. I have seen one before. It is okay I will just go now" I said backing out of the stall. "Unless...you will have a cup of coffee with me?"

"I guess Valentine; if you say it is okay. I mean I didn't shoot you or anything." He chuckled looking down at the gun. "Maybe Tokyo doesn't have to know about this. A cup of coffee sounds good. Yeah, I could use a cup for sure"

"Sounds good, if you can just point me in the direction of the chow hall I will get us that cup of coffee and we can forget this ever happened"

I walked quickly to the wooden structure they call the chow hall. It was painted like a big red barn next to the office where I first met Zak. The aroma of bacon and sausage was beginning to linger in the air. It was luck that the cooks arrived early to start breakfast. The large coffee makers were humming with fresh brew. I was able to get two coffees in Styrofoam cups and head back to the barn. I wanted to get there before any of the other rodeo clowns arrived and have a little chat with Trip. I wasn't sure if he was nervous that Tokyo would find out Trip carried a handgun or if it was that he was worried about showing it to me. Either way I needed to play this up.

If a person feels you are keeping their secret they will either keep a friendly attitude, butter you up hoping to keep your mouth shut. Or they will threaten you to keep your mouth shut just to protect their secret. I feel Trip is going to be dancing the jig just to keep me from telling Tokyo that he jumped up and pointed a gun at me this morning.

I got back to the barn and presented the coffee to Trip then took a seat on a bale of hay next to him.

"So why do they call you Trip, was it because you fell all the time, tripped over your own feet?" I chuckled trying to ease the tension in the air.

"Nah, they just started calling me Trip one day after the guys played an initiation prank on me"

"If Trip is a nickname then what is your real name?" I daringly asked.

"I am not supposed to tell Valentine, you know that"

"I heard that rumor; I just don't understand why someone's name given at birth has to be a secret"

"It is a pact we have, just like some wear the clown make-up all the time. I don't know all the facts but I hear it is because some...not me...got into a little trouble in town a while back and ...dang it, I don't know Valentine. It is just the way it is! Tokyo will be here with the guys soon so I need to start getting ready. I just cannot talk about these things" He said standing to brush off the hay.

I was making a mental list of the rodeo clowns that do not wear the all day make-up when Tokyo appeared at the door way to the stall. He sighed then started talking slowly as if I had a hearing problem.

"I...said...to...stop...asking...ques tions...Valentine!"

"We were just having coffee Tokyo, just morning coffee talk. What is the big deal?"

"I heard your conversation Valentine. Do you have a listening problem as well? If it happens again I will have to talk to Zak about your sticking your nose where it does not belong”

"I just want to fit in, make friends Tokyo, do my job, and have coffee with my fellow employees. Why do you have such a problem with that?" I said standing up. I usually don't take too kindly to threats. I like to diffuse the problem straight up and always have the upper hand, show no fear. So if standing up to Tokyo is the way to fit in around here and be respected, I am up for the challenge. I moved two steps closer and he mimicked me and moved two steps closer toward me. "I don't have a hearing problem Tokyo or a listening problem so I would appreciate a little trust. I was just being friendly so drop it!"

He stared at me with mad hate in his eyes. The feeling was very much reciprocated. I stared right back. He stood in silence, breathing so loud his nasal hair flared.

"Today you saddle Buddy on your own Valentine" he growled. Then he simply turned and left. I tossed my empty coffee cup in the garbage bin and strolled down to Buddy's stall. When I turned to go in I noticed Preacher slipping the saddle on Buddy. He put his finger to his mouth to tell me keep quiet. I nodded and started helping him tighten the straps to the saddle. He was carefully and quietly showing me how to put it on. Then came the bridle and he held it up pointing to the mouth bit then placed it in Buddy's mouth. I mouthed the words "thank You" as he turned to leave the stall.

Chapter 12

Buddy the horse gave a whinny as he turned around in his stall to face me. I was happy and deeply moved that he recognized me. We hugged for the longest time while I stroked his neck. Preacher brought me the flag as I mounted Buddy preparing for the start of the rodeo. Knowing the routine Buddy gently walked toward the arena and stopped waiting for the signal.

While waiting Preacher approached me on my left as he did the day before. I looked for Tokyo to appear on the right but he was a no show.

"Where is Tokyo today I wonder? Do you think I made him so mad he is going to skip walking out with us this morning preacher?" I asked looking down from my seat on Buddy.

"I suggest you don't try to get him all riled up Valentine. Just do your job. I saw him walk over to speak with Zak earlier"

I looked straight ahead. Maybe I am trying to get Tokyo all riled up. The rodeo has been a joy but I am ready to find information and solve a cold case. I looked around seeing no one coming so I nudged Preacher a little.

"Do you also have the mindset that no one should know your real name preacher? Same as the others?"

"Is Valentine your real name?" he said looking up at me. Good point.

"Yes it actually is Preacher and what is yours?"

"Let it go Valentine, if that is your real name. Why do you want to start trouble?"

"You see Valentine is my real name but trouble is my middle name"

I am not getting anywhere with this divide and conquer game. They all seem to be afraid of Tokyo. Maybe I should use a different tactic, come up with a plan to shake things up. I looked down at Preacher again.

"I noticed a couple of rodeo clowns sitting around a bonfire the other night. Can anyone join in or is it exclusive just for rodeo clowns?"

"It is time to ride Valentine, Zak is starting to announce. I guess if you wanted to come it would be okay. But I didn't invite you, it was your decision"

Buddy trotted out to the middle and I displayed the flag for the national Anthem then we galloped around the arena and back to the barn. I have to admit it was more amazing than I could explain. I was taking the saddle off of Buddy when Zak came in to see me.

"Valentine, you, and Buddy seem to have quite a connection. You did good out there today. The crowd loves you. I want you to help out with the roping this afternoon. You will need to change your clothes, just jeans and a western shirt. Oh and Tokyo is my trusted hand, do not piss him off, okay? Or this will be your last rodeo just like Buddy" he said tipping his hat.

"Wait, Buddy's last rodeo? What will happen to him?"

"He is still a fine horse but we are thinking we need to retire him for a trick horse. They can be expensive so we will most likely sell old Buddy here. You just be back here around five pm to help with the steers Valentine"

Grabbing the brush I started giving Buddy some much needed love. Tears were stinging my eyes and I did not know why. Just because a horse is old does not mean they have to sell him. Buddy put his big head over my shoulder as if to tell me not to worry, he will be okay. *Or he was saying take me with you,* I thought to myself. I spent extra time grooming him and filling his water trough before I left him to go back to my hotel and change.

As I am walking to my jeep I heard footsteps behind me so I wheeled around to see who may be following me. It was the rodeo clown they call Hippie, and he looked angry.

"I hear you been asking everyone personal questions Valentine and you need to stop or you will be sorry!"

"Is that a threat of some kind Hippie?" I said putting my hands on my hips and turning to face him.

"You take it however you want Valentine. Just stop! Matter of fact you should leave here and never come back if you know what is good for you!"

"You do not scare me Hippie, and you are not going to scare me away from the rodeo. Is that what you are trying to do? Why don't you tell me what you rodeo clowns are so afraid of? Because I personally think there must be something going on around here. Strangely, you are all a little too touchy with a simple question I asked just to get to know you"

He was about five feet from me. Full clown make-up on. Ironically he had a huge red smile painted on his angry face. He stepped closer one arm reared back like he was tempted to hit me but questioned himself. Most men are brought up to not hit a woman and it tortures them. "Do you want to fight me Hippie?"

"I want you to go away!" he screamed coming closer.

"Not a good idea Hippie. I am warning you, it will not end well for you" I made an attempt to warn him.

He took another step, recklessly swung his right arm too wide to punch me. Blocking his right hook with my left arm I leaned forward letting my right fist connect with his nose, watching the blood begin to spurt. He grabbed his face and stumbled back and I followed up by slamming my left fist in his ribs. I felt the familiar crack as my fist hit the target. Ironically, he fell sprawling on the ground whining like a child who stubbed a toe. He was hurt body and ego, so I stepped back and watched him roll on the ground. He didn't know whether to hold his bleeding nose or his bruised ribs. I looked around for witnesses. None around.

After a short few moments I reached down offering Hippie a hand up off the ground. He slapped it away so I took a step back ready for round two.

"Hippie, I warned you. Told you it was not a good idea. Now you have two choices"

"Shut up! Stop talking!" he yelled.

"Not until I tell you the two choices. How rude!" I said trying for a little humor and self preservation. My knuckles were starting to sting a little. "So here they are Hippie. You can get up and we shall go at it again, just let the wild bull loose as I say. Not the best choice seeing as you obviously have a bruised nose and ego. Or you can crawl, limp, or run back to your rodeo clown club and we shall never speak of this again. Now how do you see this playing out Hippie? Which choice are you going with? Choose wisely, I am no frail flower as you can see"

Hoping he would choose the second one so I do not have to pull out my revolver and reveal the fact that I am concealing a weapon. Hippie got to his feet and glared at me. I could feel the wheels turning in his head as his clown face turned sad. If he tells anyone that a girl bloodied his nose he will never live it down. He put one hand over his bleeding nose and wrapped his other arm around his waist, turned and limped off. He looked back only once before he turned the corner around the barn and was out of sight.

I turned back to finish the walk to my jeep. I am going to need ice on this fist tonight. Breaking noses hurts the knuckles. But it was so worth it.

On the drive to the hotel my mind is fast scribbling the notes of what just occurred, and what I have observed so far. Hippie is aggressive, definitely has something to hide, and hates me asking questions. He is also one that wears full clown make-up, all the time. Tokyo is frustrated that he caught Trip and I having a discussion in the hang out stall while drinking morning coffee. No clown make-up unless he is helping out in the mornings. He was a no show this morning. The ones that wear full clown make-up are Trip, Hippie, Preacher so far as I can tell. That leaves Ringo and Baby boy to check out still. Maybe I will get that chance this afternoon.

Arriving at the hotel I park two doors down right in front of the self serve ice machine. Walking in to my hotel room I grab my ice bucket and head back to the machine and fill it up keeping the plastic bag out for an ice pack later. Returning to my room I hear my phone.

"Marja? I was going to call you in a few minutes. I am in the middle of icing down my knuckles, what do you have for me?"

"Icing your knuckles Esther? Were you in a fight?" she asked.

"Yes I was in a fight with an aggressive rodeo clown who wanted me to stop asking questions. I will be okay. Did you find anything on the elusive Steven Andrew Miller for me?" I said changing the subject. I knew I should not tell Marja too much information because she will most likely pass it on to Detective Sailor and I will again have to hear how I should be more careful. "Did you find a high school picture possibly?"

"I sure did. I am sending it to your phone now. It is an old one but you can see hair color and eyes at least. How did it go with Connie Munro last night?"

"Connie was hesitant to give me any names, but told me an ex-boyfriend, who was a rodeo clown, gave her a bloody lip and Anthony Whitmore saved her. Angry and jealous could be a motive for murder"

"It is clear she must be scared. Will you go back and search her house now that we have permission?"

"I might, after I get finished stirring up the rodeo clowns. Clearly if I keep pushing someone will get upset enough to blurt out something or make a mistake? Kind of like today. I was confronted after asking questions over coffee this morning. I wish you were here Marja. I think I might bring something home after this case that is better than a foyer table"

"Are the rodeo clowns you are dealing with creepy? Clowns are scary creepy Esther. I would come down but....I am afraid of clowns. Wait what are you bringing home this time?"

"A horse named Buddy" I blurted out. I haven't even inquired about buying him yet. "Are you interested? We have plenty of room at the ranch"

"I will be there tonight Esther. No clowns will keep me away! A horse! Really? You are the best sister ever!"

"Okay, calm down. I still need to make the arrangements. I will send you the address and see you in the morning. Drive safe Marja"

"I know the address Esther; I made the hotel arrangements for you remember? Also... I may have put a tracker on your jeep...maybe. Well gotta go, see you later, bye!"

"Marja...Marja..." I knew she would hang up. Tracker on my jeep really? Marja and detective Sailor will never let me live down what happened in Mexico.

Chapter 13

I fell asleep only to wake up to a puddle the ice bag left behind. I squeezed my hands exercising them a bit and they feel fine. I still got it. It has been a while since I punched someone but I still got it. Whenever I need to make a point and make it fast I usually pull out the rifle. Allowing that red dot laser pointer dance around on their face will always get them to spill their guts. I think I will take it with me tonight for sitting around the campfire with the rodeo clowns.

Throwing on western jeans and a shirt I gathered my book bag to head over to the rodeo. I have no idea what to expect or how I can be of any help with cattle roping but I will not miss the opportunity to be there and get more information about the rest of the rodeo

clowns. After stashing my shiny red
jeep in the usual spot, I strolled over to
the horse barn. Giving Buddy a pat on
the head as I made my way to the last
stall hoping to find the guys gathering.
Sure enough I turned the corner and
three of the rodeo clowns were lying
around in the hay. Preacher, Baby Boy
and Ringo taking a siesta I assume,
before roping begins. No sign of Hippie
and his busted nose.

I have a little more time before I
am actually supposed to arrive so I
decide to have a talk with the rodeo
boss, Zak in his office. Let the clowns
sleep. As I turn to walk out of the barn I
noticed Tokyo walking in. Meeting him
half way I nod and continue. I want him
to think I learned my lesson about
asking questions. The jangling of his
spurs confirmed he continued walking.
I did not turn around. Neither did he.

Zak was at his desk when he
yelled for me to come in. I took the

chair across from him and he leaned way back in his office chair.

"Zak, you look concerned. Anything happening to make you worry?" I asked trying to give the impression of empathy.

"Nah, Valentine just same stuff, different day. I suppose you heard one of our rodeo clowns got into a scuffle. They cracked his rib, messed up his face a little; he can't ride a horse for a while. I am used to it with these guys but now I am going to be a man short. Glad you are here"

"I had not heard. Do you know who he was in a fight with?" I inquired. I did not lie exactly because I did not hear anything…except the crunch of his ribs perhaps. Maybe just a little lie. "I can fill in here if you need me boss"

"He won't tell us. Typical. Men just fight sometimes. What did you want to see me about Valentine?"

"It is about Buddy the horse. You said you are going to sell him, correct?"

"Before you get started Valentine, Buddy has still got a few more years in him. He is just not drawing any crowds. It costs us money in food and hay so we are going to sell him. You are not with a group that worries about animals are you?"

"No Zak, I want to buy Buddy. I have a little money saved up, I need a horse, and Buddy needs a new home"

"It is that simple huh?"

"It can be for the right price. I will let you think about it a while and you let me know tonight or in the morning, okay Zak?" I said bluntly.

If he raises the price because I want Buddy he will be sorry. I will contact one of those animal rights groups. Just watch and see. "I am heading out to help with roping now. Who do I see for instructions? I have never worked with cattle"

"Tokyo"

I stood up to walk out of the office and turned back one last time.

"Sorry to hear about Hippie getting hurt. I hope he heals fast"

I left him with a sour look on his fast. If he is a smart man he will figure out he never mentioned Hippie's name. Right now I need to find Tokyo. I plan on pushing some buttons around here real soon. I am growing weary of this case and these rodeo clowns.

I am fairly sure I can rule out Preacher as being the aggressive ex-boyfriend of Connie Munro. He is too helpful and kind to be a suspect. Hippie is aggressive but it could be because he was not raised up to respect women. Tokyo has been here the longest and rarely wears clown make-up. I think I can rule out Trip, he is too timid to have committed a murder. That leaves two rodeo clowns, Baby Boy and Ringo.

Time to make some clowns stumble and fall.

As I entered the barn I could hear loud voices. Tokyo was standing at the entrance to the last stall where they all hang out. His fist were pumping in the air trying to get his point across. I quickly slipped into Buddy's stall trying to listen. Buddy was nudging me for a pet so I grabbed the brush to keep him quiet. Standing there brushing Buddy listening to Tokyo berate the men.

"Someone knows who did this! I want answers, don't play dumb boys!"

I choked back a giggle. I could only imagine those manly rodeo men, bull riders, sitting in the hay, getting lectured by Tokyo. Tensions were high. I am satisfied Hippie chose to not tell anyone it was me that busted his nose. He would never live it down and Tokyo would surely have me fired for it.

Deciding it was time to show myself I gave Buddy a quick hug, whispered in his ear, and exited his stall. As I walked towards Tokyo I had a little skip in my step and a smile on my face. He scowled at me as I approached. I wish I could take credit for the injuries to Hippie but I was not ready to reveal my secret. Apparently neither was Hippie.

"Hey Tokyo, I am here to help with roping cattle I hear. Where do you want me?"

"Valentine, wipe that smile off your face. This is a serious job"

"If you say so Tokyo" I said as I brushed by him. I took a seat in the hay with the other guys showing support. As if I am part of the team even though I am a rebel at heart.

Tokyo took the opportunity to change into instructions for tonight's cattle roping competition and barked out everyone's duties. I was to be positioned at the gate and when the signal is given I jump on the gate, releasing it so the cattle can run into the arena. Then jump off the gate and push it closed with me safely inside. Baby Boy was to keep the rider safe and Ringo would be on horseback in the arena. Preacher on the other hand would fill in for Hippie who usually provides entertainment in between competitors and gets the crowd going. Hippie will have to be in the background loading the next calf into the chute. He cannot be seen in public due to his injuries.

All set with our job descriptions; we exit the barn and walk towards the arena. Hundreds of Rodeo fans were filling the stadium seats ready for a show. The rodeo Clown, Baby Boy walks with me and shows me how to work the cattle gate, jumping on to swing it open and off to push it closed.

"Be careful of the hooves and horns Valentine, they are not pets and can knock you down. They may be little and cute but those hooves can do some damage to your face if you get knocked on your bootie"

"Thank you for being concerned about my face and bootie Baby Boy. I will be careful to hold onto the gate as it swings. It sounds quite fun. Say did you grow up around here? You look familiar in some way, like we knew each other from high school perhaps"

"Listen valentine, I get that you are trying to be a friend, pal, mi Amiga but Tokyo has strict rules and we all follow them"

"Help me understand how recognizing an old friend from school is against the rules Baby Boy. I mean you are a little short in stature but isn't that just a stage name? It is hard to take anyone serious that goes by the name of Baby Boy" I said stopping to face him. I put my hand on his shoulder showing compassion. Hoping this would trigger some trust between us.

"If it is that important to you Valentine my real name is Manuel, Manny for short. I had nowhere to go when Tokyo took me in. I have to respect that, I am grateful. We all have to be one hundred percent committed or we…something bad may happen to us. Like what happened to Hippie"

"Thank you for trusting me Manny, I won't tell anyone. To ease your mind, let us just suppose what happened to Hippie was not because he talked to me or told something he wasn't supposed to. Maybe he just made a bad choice, picked a fight with the wrong cowboy…or cowgirl" I smiled and flashed a wink then turned to continue walking to the gate. I rubbed my knuckles for visual effect. Baby Boy caught up to me and pulled lightly on my arm so I would stop. He looked down at my red knuckles and started giggling and speaking something in

Spanish as he stepped back looking at me in disbelief.

I am not sure what he said but it was most likely something to do with how funny it was that a girl beat up one of the tough rodeo clowns. People swear they are some way, have an attitude, or rough personality because they are fighting inner demons, but they are actually fighting the consequences of the choices they make. You do not kick a wild hog and then act surprised when he bites you.

I put my arm around Baby Boy and we walked toward the gate in unison. The red painted smile on his face could not even compare to the real smile Baby Boy was sporting when we arrived at the cattle area and Hippie was standing there.

"Why are you two so happy is something funny? Just get to work and stop lolly gagging. You are on the gate Valentine!" Barked Hippie.

"I got it Hippie, no worries" I replied exchanging a secret smile with Baby Boy. He walked away shaking his head, still laughing and mumbling.

The cattle roping was a blast even if I did only ride the gate. The crowd was loud as they announced the winner. I stood on the gate looking at the winner parade around the arena holding his trophy high in the air. Preacher ran around as well coaxing the crowd to keep cheering. Out of the corner of my eye I saw Tokyo ride into the arena in full clown get up riding fast. He was riding Buddy. He pulled the reins hard and Buddy slid on his back hooves to a quick stop. Trip rode in the arena next and the two riders backed up their horses as music blared over the loud speakers. They were making the horses do short stops, step sideways and turns like an orchestrated dance routine. Baby Boy joined me on the gate.

"Is this trick riding or something Manny? Do they do this every night after the competitions?"

"Yes, this is why they are selling Buddy to get a stallion that can do trick riding. Poor Buddy is too old for this anymore. He breaks a leg and it is all over for him. Off to the glue factory it will be"

"I had no idea they used Buddy for this. I thought he only was ridden during the national anthem! Buddy deserves retirement. I have to fix this. This will not happen again. Not on my watch" I said jumping down from the cattle gate.

"There is nothing you can do Valentine, he is a rodeo horse. Are you coming to the bonfire tonight?"

"I will be there as soon as I check on Buddy. He is more than a rodeo horse in my eyes"

Chapter 14

Walking to the barn I hear the familiar hoof sounds trotting up behind me. I turn noticing Buddy foaming with sweat then glance up at Tokyo. He dismounts before Buddy even comes to a complete stop and offers me the reins. I see his eyes but I am sure not to meet them. I want to saddle him up and ride him till he is foaming at the mouth, the bit gouging his mouth till it bleeds.

Reluctantly I take the reins for Buddy's sake. When he recognizes me he gives a little whiny and puts his head on my shoulder as we walk slowly the rest of the way to the barn.

"That is my personal saddle Valentine, be sure it gets put away properly in the tack shed, near the bunk house. Follow my orders Valentine. You did good on the gate tonight, keep it up" Tokyo snarled. I never looked up at him, just continued to free Buddy from his saddle. I tossed it on the ground in the stall as I grabbed the brush hoping to show him I care.

Buddy was sucking up water as fast as he could. I had never seen him so sweaty. My heart was feeling much love for this horse. We connected. I will never let them treat him like this again. Animals are a lot like humans and have feelings. We don't treat the old aged humans this bad. We all need care in our old age, horses included.

Zak came into the barn and stopped briefly at Buddy's stall. I glared at him. He had white envelopes in his hand and waved them at me.

"It is pay day Valentine, come to the bunk house when you are done"

"Wait Zak, I will be there in a few minutes but I just want to let you know I am taking Buddy tomorrow after he rides in the National Anthem. You can loan me a horse trailer for a day and I will return it"

"Well I haven't come up with a price yet Valentine; I will let you know in the morning. Meet me at the bunkhouse; it is where I hand out checks" He nodded and left the barn.

"I will not take no for an answer", I whispered to Buddy. He seemed to know what I said as he shook his head, stomped his hoof and gave a big whiny. I put the brush away and picked up the saddle to carry with me to the bunkhouse.

Never been to the bunkhouse so I wandered towards the second barn where they keep the horses ridden by the rodeo clowns. The saddle was not light so I grabbed it by the horn and dragged it part way. It is not my job to do his dirty work, if he does not like the way I carry his saddle then he can do it his self.

I found the tack room behind the bunk house and tossed the saddle in then shut the door. Something caught my eye. I opened the door again and went in to look around. Taking a further look around I see books on a shelf full of dust. The shelf was about height with photo albums all lined up. I pulled one down and brushed off the dust. Flipping through it I saw pictures of a younger Tokyo, several rodeo queens, a younger picture of Buddy the horse, rodeo clowns holding up bottles of liquor in some sort of celebration.

And then I noticed a picture of a man about the size and body shape of Hippie or Ringo, no clown make-up, with a dark haired woman. The man had his arm tightly around her pulling her toward him. She was sporting a black eye and was not posing like the proud loving girlfriend. Her arms were crossed, pouting lip and angry eyes as if she was being forced to stand for the picture. I slipped it out of the album and put it in my pocket. The high school photo that Marja sent me of Steven Andrew Miller was still in a file on my phone. I opened the file trying to compare the two men. It looked like it could possibly be a match. I must be getting close. I returned the album and headed to the door way of the bunk house. Zak standing in the middle of the small room giving a rundown of the night's events still holding on to the envelopes with everyone's pay.

I slowly looked at the room taking it in. There were three sets of bunk beds lining the far wall. The floors were cheaply tiled and walls painted light gray. Each bunk had a red plaid blanket all neatly made. *"Tokyo must run a tight ship"* I thought to myself. There was a small kitchen to the right of the doorway and a large table and chairs in the middle of the room. Preacher and Tokyo had on no make-up. Both were leaning against a set of bunks. Baby Boy and Trip were sitting at the table with a deck of cards. Also no make-up Hippie was lying on the top bunk. I could tell by the bandages across his nose. I stepped further into the room looking for Ringo but he was no where around.

After the paychecks were handed out everyone headed to the bon fire behind the barns. I caught Zak by the arm of his shirt and looked him in the eye. I had on my serious face so he stopped briefly.

"I know valentine, I will give you an answer in the morning do not worry so much"

"I am worried. Buddy deserves to retire and I know just the place. I am taking him in the morning Zak so get yourself prepared" I said letting go of his sleeve.

I turned around and most all the rodeo clowns had left the bunk house leaving Hippie behind. I glanced around the room but nothing seemed to be out of place. Plus I cannot do a good search with Hippie on the top bunk, so I decided to head out to the bon fire.

The one they call Ringo was stoking the fire then passed out cans of beer from a cooler. Large logs circled the fire and most of the rodeo clowns were sitting on them watching the fire and opening their pay envelopes. The one they called Preacher started strumming an acoustic guitar. I had all the rodeo clowns in one spot, drinking, guards down… so now may be the time to stir up the crowd and see who spills their secrets.

I took a seat on the log nearest Ringo hoping to strike up a conversation. He is the only one I have not had an opportunity to talk to.

"Ringo, I don't think we have had a chance to talk since I started with the rodeo, how long have you been with

this group?" I asked. He glared. A chill
ran down my spine. There is something
not quite right here I can feel it. "I saw
you riding this evening, have you been
riding long?"

"Have you been this nosy for long
Valentine? If you are assuming I want
to have a conversation with you then
you are very wrong! I know your type
trying to be all cute and nice. Just go
have a seat somewhere else. Women do
not belong here! I have nothing to say
to you" He snapped.

"Wow Ringo, let me see if I have
this correct. I come over here where we
are all enjoying the bon fire together,
and you get rude just because I asked
you how long you have been riding." I
looked straight at him as he turned to
look away ignoring me. Like I was
disgusting to look at. "I assumed
nothing by coming to talk to you except
that we all work for the rodeo and we
are simply hanging out. I do not have

cooties Ringo nor do I have any agenda"
I finished. I heard a slight chuckle from
across the circle and saw Baby Boy
covering his mouth to squelch a full out
laugh. Ringo sat perfectly still staring at
the fire. I turned back facing the fire as
well. A quiet moment went by; even
Preacher stopped playing the guitar.
Tokyo stood up watching me, daring me
to start asking questions. I got the
distinct impression everyone stared at
me and Ringo as though they expected
a bomb to go off any minute. All was
quiet except for the crackling of the fire.
It was absurd. Are we supposed to just
sit and never talk or would they all be
talking if a woman was not in their
presence. What does that even mean?

I tried to focus on the fire even
though I was trembling with frustration
and anxiety. Ringo must be the time
bomb, the one in the group who is
mean as a snake. The one who only
comes out at night. I could kick myself

for taking this case. I can understand why it went cold with everyone being so uptight. I stared at the fire in resignation that I was not getting anywhere with Ringo. Not tonight. I looked around the campfire and can fairly say no one has my interest as a suspect yet and the feeling of wasting my time undercover was creeping up on me. I wish I could say I shook it off and let it go, but I knew it was inevitable, I would not.

Ringo stood up briefly to throw a little more wood on the fire and as he sat down I tilted my head to look at him.

"What did you mean by saying women do not belong here Ringo? Like here at the bon fire or here as in the rodeo or did you mean the entire world should be included in your hate of women?" I said sarcastically. I braced myself for his response. I had poked the sleeping bear. On purpose. He stood up. A tactic I was familiar with. He wanted to tower over me so I would fear him. I stood up and turned to face him.

"I'm waiting for your answer Ringo" I said folding my arms, showing no fear, daring him to speak.

"Valentine!" yelled Tokyo trying to diffuse the tension in the air.

My eyes never left Ringo. Never look away; it will give them an opportunity to sucker punch. No I kept my eyes focused on Ringo. He slowly looked up peering from under the rim of his cowboy hat. His eyes were glazed over, his lips trembling.

"I do not have a problem hitting a woman especially if it is to shut her up Valentine. Just ask any of these guys who have known me a long time" He said in a low growl. He shifted his weight, his fists were clenched tightly. I recognized the body language. I took a slight step back so to be out of his arm reach. The fist swing would not make contact unless he stepped toward me. I planned how my first punch would land on the left side of his jaw. I envisioned him wincing from the pain as I slam my left fist in an upper cut sending his head flying back while I sweep his feet out from under him. Ready to rumble.

A rough hand clasped down on my shoulder and I turned slightly to see Tokyo standing next to me.

"Valentine, time to move over here" He pointed to the other side of the fire. "Go sit on the other side of the bon-fire or get out of here. Ringo is not one to mess with" He said calmly and firmly. Deciding it was best to not show my hand seeing that nobody knows that I was the one that gave Hippie the bloody nose, I walked around the fire and sat next to Baby Boy. Manny, my only friend at the rodeo.

Chapter 15

Baby Boy tried to put me in a different mood but my anger was raging inside me. Realizing Tokyo actually tried to diffuse the situation with Ringo pleased me. I think he is starting to accept me into the group. Manny, the one they call Baby Boy, nudged me and I looked over at him as he stuck out his tongue trying to humor me. It made me relax a little. Preacher was picking his guitar, Tokyo was lighting a cigar, Trip was knocking back a few cans of cheap beer, and Ringo just stared at the fire like a brooding child.

The humor lies in the fact that I am sitting around a bon-fire with five grown men of which four of them are still sporting full clown-make-up, I had to laugh. Imagine if you can, the flames of a burning fire dancing off men with clown faces. It is the stuff nightmares are made of. I am living that nightmare.

Beginning to feel a ferocious headache coming on, I told Baby Boy I was going to turn in for the night. I stood giving a slight wave to the guys and noticed Ringo had a knife out whittling on a stick. I made a mental note of the possible weapon and turned to leave. Baby Boy decided to walk back to the barn with me so I could tell Buddy the horse good night. He had drunk a few of those cheap beers as well so as we walked he began to talk freely and wobble slightly.

"Ringo is a bad egg Valentine. You don't want to mess with him" He slurred.

"I would only mess with him if he messed with me Baby Boy. I could feel his resentment toward me just because I am a woman"

"I hear rumor is that Ringo hit his girlfriend and got into some trouble, right here at the rodeo. Tokyo protects him like a son. I just ignore him; he is probably the reason we have to wear clown make-up all day and only allowed to wash it off at night”

“Wait so you all wash it off before bed and do not sleep in it”

“Gosh no Valentine, it would smear on the pillows you crazy girl!”

“So if something happened like an emergency in the middle of the night, you would all run out with a clean face?” I asked.

Baby Boy stopped in his tracks and faced me trying not to sway. I put my hand on his shoulder to steady him.

“What kind of emergency Valentine? I mean what are you thinking dear. Is that your plan to see us without our clown make-up, why is that so important to you?”

“Baby Boy, you do not have to worry it is not like I am going to set the barn on fire, but I could pretend there is a fire so you all run out" I joked.

Baby Boy scrunched up his face and shook his head.

"No Valentine, what are you up to anyway? You ask questions all the time, want to know everyone's name…I am sensing you are not who you say you are?" He asked curiously.

"Come in to see Buddy with me, then we can talk more privately" I said tucking my arm in his. I do not plan on confiding with Baby Boy but after a few drinks I may get information out of him and possibly he won't remember it in the morning hopefully. It was a chance I was willing to take. It is a better plan than starting a fire in the barn anyway.

We entered the barn and slipped into Buddy's stall not bothering to turn on any light. I guided Baby Boy to a bale of hay and we sat down in the dark. If he knows anything about Steven Andrew Miller I needed to find

out. I slung my arm around Baby Boys'
shoulder so we could keep our voices
down.

"Are you hitting on me
Valentine? I mean I am okay with that
but I didn't think I was your type" he
chuckled.

"No, I am not hitting on you
Baby Boy, hush and listen. I have a
friend named Connie Munro. She was
seeing a man that worked for the rodeo
named Steven. He did her wrong and I
am trying to find him. I took this job
here so I could let her know his
whereabouts. Do you know which rodeo
clown is Steven?" I asked in a low voice.
Hoping that I did not have to reveal
anything about the murder just yet.
"And if I had a type Baby Boy it would
be you, definitely you. So can you help
me out?" I lied smiling. Smiling and
lying, whatever works?

"Well I don't know anyone's real
name Valentine, except Preacher...I

think his name is Dale because I heard Zak call him that one time handing out the pay envelopes. Oh and I think Ringo's name is Sam. He has it written on the bottom of his boots. He is mean as a snake. His name should have been snake" he said starting to laugh.

"I think we are done here Baby Boy, I mean Manny. The alcohol has gone to your brain. Can you make it back to the bunk house on your own?"

"I have done it a million times deary. You cannot work, eat, or sleep around here without a little alcohol to calm your nerves and make you forget everything"

I gave Buddy a rub and walked Baby Boy out to the edge of the barn, pointed him in the right direction and turned to walk to my jeep. It was late and I was a tired cattle gate riding cowgirl. Time for bed. My nerves were on edge. Every part of my body was hurting.

As I rounded the fence surrounding the rodeo I could see the fire still burning behind the barn and Ringo and Tokyo were still staring at it.

I hopped in my jeep and drove to the hotel. I don't feel like I can crack this cold case with all the rodeo clowns keeping their secrets. I will return in the morning to carry the flag, and then make arrangements for Buddy to be transferred to the ranch. Then I might just go talk to Mrs. Whitmore again and tell her it is still a cold case.

Tucked into bed after parking two doors down and securing the locks, pushing the chair up to the door knob and propping the pillows I decided to pull out the police file one last time. There is no record of Connie Munro giving the name of her ex-boyfriend anywhere. It makes me wonder if a page of the report is missing. My head is fuzzy from the standoff with Ringo tonight. He had a knife. It would have been a messy situation.

Marja should arrive in the morning and I will be glad to have someone to talk to. I miss detective Sailor even though I am too stubborn to admit it. My hand reached for the phone to call him, but I changed my mind. Let him call me if he wants to talk or know what is happening. I have no reason to chase after him. Truth is I need him far more than he needs me.

For the first time in a long time sleep did not favor me. I tossed and turned seeing faces of clowns in my dreams. I opened one eye slightly to see daylight peeking around the edges of the curtains and decided to head to the shower. Just as I finished and wrapped a towel around my head there was a knock on the hotel door.

"Esther, are you up yet? It's me Marja, open the door!"

I hurried to move the chair lodged under the door knob and flung open the door.

"Sister! I am so glad you are here. What time is it?"

"I left early to beat the traffic Esther, and there was none so here I am at 6am arriving at your door, crazy huh?" Marja said cheerfully. "I came bearing gifts from Detective Sailor"

I took the box from her hands and we gave each other a long hug before I opened it. It was nice to have a friendly face. This case has me on edge.

"Donuts! Blueberry donuts!" I cheered loudly. "Detective Sailor sent me my favorite donuts, I am so happy"

"He came by the ranch last night and insisted I stop and pick up the donuts on the way to you. He handed me a twenty dollar bill. I kept the change. He will never ask for it. Sit down Esther, eat a donut and I will call for coffee delivery from room service"

Marja and I sat on the beds laughing and eating donuts till we were stuffed. I told her all about Buddy the horse, the rodeo clowns, punching Hippie in the nose and filled her in on what happened at the camp fire last night.

"You are so brave Esther, but I am glad it ended with Tokyo stopping you. Especially if Ringo had a knife. I will enjoy watching you carry the flag but I don't think I can handle seeing the rodeo clowns up close. Clowns send shivers up my spine. They are not cute or funny at all. It is a mask they wear to hide their true identity if you ask me"

"Clowns can be quite scary Marja, I dreamed about them all night, it was awful"

"Then I will be sitting with the crowd in the stands while you ride this morning. Oh and I located a horse trailer for sale or rent locally. We can have it delivered to the rodeo if you want. I just have to call and give them a time. I am so excited. This is better than you bringing me a piece of furniture for the ranch Esther!"

"I think we should purchase the trailer if it is in fair shape. We may need it in the future for Buddy. I do not see us coming back here to return it"

"So are you officially giving up on the case Esther?"

"I can count on one hand the amount of times I wanted to give up on a cold case this badly. I am surrounded by men dressed as clowns who disrespect women and it makes me so angry all the time. Detective Sailor and I have barely talked over this case. I think it is best I stop and talk to Mrs. Whitmore and let her know this afternoon that I cannot find her husband's murderer. I do not want to end up shooting a clown over nothing"

"I understand completely big sis, let me go over all you have learned and see if I can find something you missed then let us get ready to rescue Buddy the horse. I told mother on the phone last night and even she was excited. She is traveling through Oregon right now, but says she will be home by the end of the week to meet the new addition to the family”

"That is exactly what I need is for the family to be all together at the ranch. It will be a nice change from the rodeo. I will get ready. Wait till you see my outfit!" I gushed. "Blue fringe and all!"

Marja began spreading out the notes I had taken on the second bed along with the police file and the pictures I took at the Munro house.

"So Anthony Whitmore did buy the house for his girlfriend Connie Munro after all” she yelled to me. "I wonder if he had a last will and testament that states he leaves her the house. That would prove that Mrs.

Whitmore knew about the affair" she continued.

I stuck my head around the corner from the bathroom to look at Marja. "Would it matter if she knew Marja?" I asked.

"That would mean she lied to you. If she lied about that then what else is she lying about Esther?"

"Are you saying that possibly Mrs. Whitmore lied to me about having knowledge of the affair to take the focus off of her somehow Marja?"

"How can you be sure she is not the one who went to the mistress's home and killed her own husband?"

"He was shot, then his tongue was brutally cut out and someone watched him suffer, bleed, and die. I do not picture the soft spoken southern Mrs. Whitmore doing that, but anything is possible. Let's look back over the coroner's report when we get back"

Chapter 16

Marja gathered the files from the bed, her lap top, and snacks to stuff them in my back pack. She tucked the small .38 snub nose I gave her in it as well. We decided it was best if she carried it today for me. I had been leaving it in the jeep while working, but I have a strong feeling I may need it close to me today. Marja also brought some cash to pay for Buddy and the horse trailer. We have a plan to take Buddy the horse whether Zak has decided or not. His poor treatment ends today. We are taking him home.

On the ride over to the rodeo Marja pulled out the coroners notes and read them aloud. I love that she has the brains and I am the brawn. I might just consider taking her on my next case. I enjoy having her around.

"This report from the medical examiner states the subject, Anthony Whitmore, had a subtle hemorrhage in the facial area that was inconsistent with a fall. On the cheekbone and jaw were small faint fracture lines consistent with a blow to the face. When someone lands on the back of the skull like the subject did after a gunshot wound, you will find some injury to the front of the brain as well, because the brain bounces to the front after the skull hits the ground and stops. He had a fracture to the back of his skull as well as some blood pooling Esther"

"What are you saying Marja? Mr. Whitmore was punched in the face, and then shot in the stomach, and then they cut out his tongue?"

"Exactly. So it was possibly more than one person in on the murder that day. Most likely it was someone he knew because he had no defensive wounds and nothing under his finger nails, except a black substance that was never identified"

"That does put a new twist on things Marja" I exclaimed. Taking in the information from a new view I wonder if it could have been two rodeo clowns in on the murder of Anthony Whitmore. Tokyo was very protective of Ringo, maybe they were both in on it. I just cannot put my finger on a motive It had to be more than just jealousy.
"Thanks for looking that over again. Sometimes that medical jargon doesn't make sense to me"

"I find the only time of the day my mind is truly occupied Esther is when I am pouring over research and learning something new. I am nerdy like that. Who knew?" She laughed.

We were both laughing as we pulled into the rodeo gate. I parked my jeep next to the barn as usual and handed Marja the keys. She will need to

put the jeep in position when the man
with the horse trailer comes.

Saying Marja was excited to meet
Buddy was an understatement. We
headed straight to the barn and
Buddy's stall. Buddy instantly loved
Marja. There was lots of hugging and
petting. Preacher showed up bringing
me Buddy's saddle and he allowed
Marja and I to put it on. With a lot of
encouraging instructions we managed
to place the saddle ready for our
opening ceremony.

"Lucky day for you to come to
the rodeo Marja" Preacher said. "It is
also fair day today. There will be games
like ring toss, baseball throw and
balloon darts as well as cotton candy.
Heck, I can smell the popcorn in the air
already" he chuckled. "I love popcorn"

I smiled at Preacher. It was kind
of him to be nice and welcoming to my
little sister. I feel sure he is not involved
in the Whitmore murder; my instincts

tell me he doesn't have the personality for murder, and he loves popcorn. It is fair to rule him out. So far I have ruled out Baby Boy, Preacher, and Trip as possible suspects among the rodeo clowns. Tokyo does not wear the clown make-up and he is protective, not hiding. That leaves Hippie and Ringo. Both are extremely rude, disrespectful, and have obvious anger issues. It had to be someone that had a connection with Anthony Whitmore and his lover Connie Munro. The murder was brutal and tortuous. Someone had a grudge.

Shaking the thoughts from my head and placing them in a *'to be looked at later file somewhere deep in my brain'*, I mounted Buddy for the ride during the National Anthem. Sending Marja to the stands to sit with the crowd, Preacher handed me the flag and we walked to the arena gate to wait for our signal. Usually having two rodeo clowns escort me, I looked down from my saddle and noticed Preacher on one side and Ringo had scurried up on the other side. He reached for Buddy's bridle. We looked at each other briefly before I nudged Buddy just slightly and he took a step forward shaking his head. Ringo pulled his hand back and glared up at me.

Ringo's appearance this early in the day surprised me. He is usually only a night time rodeo clown that does trick riding and lasso competitions. It is rather bold of him to be my escort, but I am sure his intention was to aggravate me and push my buttons.

Zak finished his announcing and we got the signal to enter the arena. I gave Buddy the usual gentle kick and he startled throwing his head back and whinnied. Leaning forward, I put my hand on his neck to comfort him and noticed Ringo way too close with his spurs. Instinctively without thinking I reached over and gave his cowboy hat a

flip watching it fly into the air. As Ringo
ran after his hat I nudged Buddy into
the arena. I glanced over at Preacher
and noticed his big approving smile
turn into a chuckle. I am sure I will be
hearing about this later from one angry
Ringo the rodeo clown. But for now...we
ride!

Buddy was prancing in the ring
like never before, I swear he was
smiling. I waved to the fans and spotted
Marja waving bigger than anyone. After
our moment in the spotlight I aimed
Buddy for the barn and he took off in
the most beautiful gallop as the crowd
cheered. The rodeo clowns usually stay
behind for a little entertainment of the
crowd before the next event starts so I
knew I had time before Ringo plans his
revenge. I took the saddle off Buddy
and grabbed the brush keeping busy
occasionally looking out for anyone to
come in unexpectedly.

As I anticipated Preacher entered the barn and headed to the back stall followed by Ringo. Ringo stopped at my stall with hostility in his eyes.

"What kind of crap you trying to pull Valentine! Don't think you are getting away with treating me like this!" he bellowed opening the stall door.

Suddenly Zak appeared and Ringo hesitated a moment. I stepped forward and shut the gate catching Ringo by surprise. I get the impression he did not want to push the matter in front of Zak the boss so I struck up a conversation with Zak and invited him in the stall.

"Zak, I have purchased a small horse trailer that will be delivered here within the hour. It is time to have a serious talk"

"Today Valentine? I am a man short because of Hippie and his busted ribs and now you want me to be a horse short? How are we going to do the

National Anthem tomorrow the last day of the rodeo for another week?" He complained.

Looking over at Ringo just hanging around Zak turned to notice him as well. "Is there something you need Ringo? Why are you here anyway?" asked Zak shaking his head.

"Listen Zak, I need to take Buddy…I am going to take Buddy. The riders at night mistreat him" I said glancing over at Ringo. "Name your price and you can go out right now and buy that trick horse you so desire" I pleaded. I always give a person the opportunity to do the right thing before I come down harder. "Did I mention I have cash?"

"Ok Valentine, I will say I want…need…um…how about $1500 cash for Buddy and you can take him. But I do not know what you are going to ride tomorrow if you take him today" Zak said finally throwing his hands in the air and turning to leave. "Meet me in the office in half an hour with the cash"

"Thank you Zak, and am I off for the rest of the day. I have a few errands to run" I hollered after him.

As he was leaving Ringo appeared in the doorway to the stall. He must have been waiting just around the corner out of sight until Zak left. His legs spread in a fighting stance, hands on his hips like a gun slinger about to have a shoot out. I remembered seeing him with a knife at the campfire so I was prepared for whatever he was about to do. I stepped in front of Buddy who obviously did not like Ringo being in his stall and kept nudging me with his head.

Abruptly Marja came running into the barn yelling my name. As she turned into Buddy's stall she came face to face with Ringo who had turned to see who was running up on him.

Whipping his knife from his pocket he stood facing her with the knife in the air as if he was ready to stab someone. Marja froze. Her face went from happy to startled and scared in a quick second. She stood there not moving, staring at Ringo in his clown make-up.

"Marja, it is okay. Just walk towards me. He will not hurt you. I promise. Just walk toward me" I said softly. I inched forward to take her by the arm, keeping an eye on Ringo the whole time.

"He...It is a...clown. He is a clown. I do not like clowns" Marja stuttered as she stood frozen.

"He is a rodeo clown Marja. He will not hurt you. Let us go see Buddy the horse. Come this way" I tugged at her arm. She broke her stare long enough to look at me with tears forming in her eyes. She was still not moving, so I snapped my fingers in her face. "Marja, snap out of it. Look at me. Only me. Come in the stall with Buddy and me. Don't look at the big scary clown who is holding a knife" I started saying loudly in a sing song voice. Hoping someone may be in ear shot. "He is going to put the knife away right now. He will not hurt my little sister or I will kill him. Just walk this way" I continued. Marja stared at me and followed my voice until she was against the back wall. I shoved her down on a bale of hay then quickly turned back toward Ringo.

I reached for my revolver then quickly noticed Tokyo standing there with one arm on Ringo. Ringo put the knife away and threw me an *"I will deal with you later"* glance and the two of them walked away without saying a word. I turned back toward Marja with her big brown eyes looking lost.

"It is okay now Marja. Let us get Buddy and go home to the ranch. He will not bother us again"

"I am sorry I froze Esther, clowns are so scary. Who in their right mind would think a clown is a good thing to be. Kids don't like clowns, I don't like clowns. Geez, my heart is beating fast. I would hate to run into him in the dark. Yes, let us get Buddy and go. I will call the horse trailer people telling them to come now…right now"

"Good idea. You stay here and wait for the horse trailer people and I will go pay Zak for Buddy" I explained.

I grabbed the book bag and rushed out of the barn toward the office. If I do not leave now, get away from Ringo and this rodeo, one of us is going to jail for murder. It is not going to be me.

Chapter 17

As I am rushing to the office to pay Zak for the horse, I hear Baby Boy rushing toward me calling my name. I slowed to let him catch up to me but continued walking.

"Valentine what happened. I was napping in the bunk room and Tokyo came in practically dragging Ringo. They were screaming at each other and your name was mentioned"

"I really don't have time to explain Baby Boy; I need to see Zak in the office. I am taking Buddy the horse with me today. I do not know if I will be back" I stopped to face him. He was always kind to me so he deserved an explanation I did not want to give. "I loved working with you Baby Boy, I mean Manny. Take care of yourself"

I turned and continued toward the office glancing back at Baby Boy

who was making gestures with his
balled fists as if he was crying big clown
tears. I shook my head laughing and
entered the office. Zak was in the back
room and yelled he would be out in a
minute. I walked around looking at all
the pictures of rodeos past hanging on
the walls of the office. Some faces did
not look familiar at all. If only I knew
for sure what they all looked like
without the clown get up on.

Zak came in and I counted out
fifteen hundred in cash and laid it on
his desk. His eyes got big as he picked
up the stack and started to count it.

"It is all there I assure you Zak.
Now I will need a bill of sale and any
paperwork on Buddy from your files"

"Give me a minute Valentine.
How did you come up with this much
cash anyway?" he said looking up at me
over his glasses. "To be honest I
assumed you were bluffing about

buying the horse. I will get you that bill of sale" he said shaking his head.

"Clearly, I was not bluffing. My horse trailer will be here any minute. Please hurry because I do not want to leave my little sister alone for too long. Ringo is…well he is a really awful human being. I do not trust him" I said thinking twice about saying too much.

"Valentine we give men a second chance here. Some are rough around the edges. Some have done time. Tokyo keeps them in line" He said handing me the paperwork. "Don't you believe in second chances Valentine?"

"I believe in second chances if they are remorseful, done their time and have turned over a new leaf Zak. What I do not believe in is harboring a fugititive or covering up a murder" I blurted out. "I think there is more going on here than just second chances"

His eyes said it all. Zak knew and now I just blurted out that I knew.

I need to leave and get far away. I will take Buddy home and do some thinking. If there is a way to solve this cold case or more evidence appears I will return possibly.

"I am leaving Zak" I said sternly looking in his eyes. "Let us just part ways with no funny business. By the way, if you do not already know…Let me just inform you, I know who punched Hippie in the face" I leaned down with both hands on the desk looking him in the eyes.

"It was me!"

I turned and storming out of his office, I slammed the door behind me. Heading toward the barn I can see the horse trailer Marja ordered backing up to the barn and a crowd forming. A crowd of rodeo clowns. I picked up my pace thinking the worst was happening. Marja will be terrified; I have to get to her. I pushed past Trip and Preacher as I entered the barn. Turning into the second stall where I left Marja and Buddy I stopped in my tracks. I busted out laughing. Marja was sitting on Buddy bareback with Baby Boy holding the reins.

"Look at me, I found a nice friendly clown and I am riding Buddy" Marja grinned.

"Okay maybe this friendly clown whose name is Baby Boy, will help us load up Buddy. The horse trailer is here Marja. Time to go"

I agreed to pay the men to haul the horse trailer and Buddy to the ranch. Marja has her car still at the hotel and I have to pack up the hotel. Marja called Detective Sailor who agreed to reluctantly meet the horse trailer at the ranch.

"He did not ask to speak to me Marja?" I asked timidly.

"He asked if you were okay and if you were coming home but he did not ask to speak to you. Are you two going to break up or something Esther?”

"I hope not Marja. I think we just need to have some long talks when I get back. I will fix it. I love him Marja” I sniffled. “I was so wrapped up in this case there was no room left for him. I realize now just how much he means to me. I will never let that happen again”

"He did buy you donuts Esther”
"Yes he did”

Buddy loaded in the horse trailer as if he knew he was going to be taken to a nice place. He was happy to leave his ten by ten stall that was his home for years. We threw a little hay in there for the trip and waved good-bye.

Straight away I spun around to see all the rodeo clowns facing me. All except Ringo. I scanned their clown faces trying to take it all in. I can see the draw to the rodeo life. Being around horses, entertaining the crowds is all a good thing for some. Especially those that have nowhere to go or deserve a second chance in life. The rodeo gives them a purpose and a family. I will miss Preacher and Baby Boy for sure; I will cherish their kindness and their trust in me. Trip is timid and holds back his emotions but he did share a coffee with me.

Saying good-bye is never easy in any situation. I want to say the right thing but the words do not always present themselves. I settled for a hug from Baby Boy and Preacher, whispering in each ear to stay safe and take care. I waved at Trip and Tokyo who gave me a nod. I was glad Ringo and Hippie chose to stay away. I hope to never see them again.

Marja and I walked to the jeep and headed for the hotel. Our plan was to drive straight to the ranch to get there right after Buddy arrived. As we sat on the bed gathering our things my inner radar went off. Something was nagging at me about this case. I have never given up on a cold case before, so I am hoping that is all it is.

Marja sat on the bed next to me and put her arm around me. Sensing something was on my mind.

"Something wrong Esther or you just hate leaving the rodeo behind?" Marja asked in her soft voice. "We could come back as spectators sometime but no clowns please" she laughed.

"It is okay to be afraid of clowns Marja. When I was young I was afraid of monsters. I thought monsters lived in my closet and under my bed. I would wedge a chair under the closet door knob so they could not come out and get me at night" I explained. "I have never told anyone that before"

"I am glad you shared that with me Esther. I miss you when you are on a case. I am sure Detective Sailor does too. Everything is going to be great

when we get back to the ranch. I hope
Buddy likes his new home"

"I am not going straight back to
the ranch Marja. There is still
something I have to do. I am worried
about something Baby Boy told me. I
am sorry but do you think you can
head back without me?"

"I found my way here, I can find
my way back Esther. What should I tell
detective Sailor, he is waiting for us?"

"Tell him I miss him and I will be
home soon. I will be in touch"

"I do not like the sound of that
Esther. I can stay if you like?"

"I need to do this for me. I
cannot give up just yet. I have to try
one more thing. Go home and enjoy
Buddy little sis"

I walked Marja out to her car
that was parked two doors down on the
opposite side I was parked. I taught her
well. I waved good-bye and watched her
drive away then went back into the

hotel and put all my belongings in the back pack. I checked out of the hotel and got in the jeep. It is approximately twenty five minutes to Round Rock, I will start there. The Whitmore's have to know something. Mrs. Whitmore lied to me about knowing her husband had an affair. She doesn't need to protect a dead man's reputation so why did she lie? I am about to find out. She at least owes me the truth after what I went through. On every cold case there is a fibster lurking in the shadows.

I arrive at the Whitmore residence in Round Rock before noon and knock on the door. After a few moments Summer Whitmore answered the door.

"Hello Summer do you remember me, I am Esther Valentine. Your mom is not expecting me but is she in so we can have a chat?"

"Yes she is napping though, should I go wake her up for you?" she said hesitantly.

"Well how about you and I have a little talk and maybe she will wake up soon. Do you have anything to drink, maybe some water or tea?"

"We could have a tea party if you like. Mommy lets me make tea in the automatic tea maker sometimes"

"That sounds wonderful. I will wait in the living room while you go prepare the tea" I encouraged her.

While Summer was busy in the kitchen making us tea, I wandered around the house a bit. Checked the drawers in the office then headed up stairs. At the top of the stairs I could hear rock music playing and I assumed it was Winter the older sister. I tapped on the door lightly and listened. The music went quiet but no one came to the door. I knocked again.

"Go away you little twerp, you cannot come in" said the voice from inside the room.

I checked the knob and it was unlocked so I let myself in.

"Hello Winter, I am Esther Valentine and I work for you mom April Whitmore. Mind if we have a chat?"

"Why are you in my room? You can't just come in my room. I thought it was my little sister knocking" Winter protested.

"See Winter we did not have a chance to meet when I was here last time, so I thought you might want to come down for a little tea party with me and your sister?" I inquired scanning the room. I knew she would not agree to a tea party with her sister. "Nice room you have, so what kind of music did I hear you playing?"

"Get out. I know who you are. You are looking into daddy's murder aren't you? Mother hired you to snoop around; well you are not going to find anything here so just go please!"

"I can't do that dear, see I am interested in your whole family. What you like, what you don't like. It will help me find your father's murderer. You have some interesting pictures on the wall here Winter, do you know all these people?"

"Get out, where is my mother! Mother! Get her out of here!" she yelled.

Soon, April Whitmore walked in the room, obviously shocked to see me standing there of course. I smiled her way. She had on a silk bathrobe over a long silk gown. A bit strange for an afternoon nap. My guess is she never got up and never dressed today.

"Esther Valentine, why are you here? Better yet why are you in my daughter's room?" She asked looking rather worried.

"I am sorry I showed up unannounced but I needed to see you.

So I see your daughter likes the rodeo. I can tell by the pictures on her wall"

"Of course she does, her father was in the rodeo" she said in a huff.

I walked over to one picture that had rodeo clowns posing around a fire. I pointed to it and looked over at Winter.

"Can you name everyone in this picture Winter?"

"Yes, but that is none of your business. Why do you ask?"

"Is one of the clowns in these pictures a Ringo the rodeo clown? Maybe the one that has his arm around you perhaps?"

She just glared at me. She looked at her mother then back at me. I turned to Mrs. Whitmore.

"I think you and your daughter need to come down stairs with me so we can talk. Then perhaps you both can explain why you have lied to me" I said firmly.

Mrs. Whitmore waved at her daughter to follow. Winter had a brief stomping fit to show her reluctance but they both followed me down stairs just as Summer Whitmore brought us all tea on a tray and set it down on the wagon wheel coffee table. No one seemed to notice I slipped the picture from the wall into the pocket of my cargo pants. I may need it later.

Chapter 18

I took a seat on the cow hide covered couch; Winter sat at the end of the couch and curled her legs up to her chest in a pouting position. Summer served everyone tea then took a seat on the floor. April Whitmore sat in the chair across from me. She kept fiddling with her robe and shifting around in the chair, not making good eye contact.

"Well Esther you have us all here so what do you want to talk about?" Mrs. Whitmore snarled.

I took a sip of tea then placed the cup on the coffee table. I glanced at everyone in the room before I began.

"Seeing that it has been two years since Mr. Whitmore died, …um was murdered, I suppose you have seen his last will and testament, am I right Mrs. Whitmore?"

"Well it was handled by our lawyers but yes I suppose I have. Why does it matter Esther?"

"Well it matters because you told me that you were not aware of his infidelity, a mistress he kept. You lied. Why did you lie to me Mrs. Whitmore?"

Mrs. Whitmore glanced at the children then back at me. It was not a family secret or she would have told me the truth in private the last time I visited. She hesitated with her answer and when she started to speak, she was interrupted by her daughter.

"Because that woman, Connie was a whore and only wanted Daddy's money!! It was embarrassing the way he acted. Daddy destroyed everything! Our family, my boyfriend...everything!! I hate him!" Winter screamed.

Mrs. Whitmore tried to hush her daughter, but it was too late. She glanced over at me then folded her hands and stared into her lap, sinking down into her chair. It is a fine line between love and hate. I am sure Winter loved her father but hated his choices.

"Winter, let us change the subject a minute. When did you start this whole look you have going on? I notice that your mother and sister have blonde hair yet you dye yours black. It is odd that you pick gothic attire because it describes mystery, horror, and gloom. Are you mysterious or are you gloomy?"

I was trying to get her angry so she will continue to blurt out. You can get quite a bit of information from a gloomy angry teenager. She did not answer me; she was too busy picking the nail polish from her fingernails. Mrs. Whitmore cleared her throat.

"She says she is in mourning. This started after her father died. It doesn't mean anything mysterious

Esther I am sure" she commented looking at her daughter.

"Well how about another question for Winter Whitmore. Were you allowed to date? Were you dating a rodeo clown at one time? Perhaps your father put a stop to it and it made you very angry with him, does that sound right?"

This sparked something in her. She roared out with anger like a tiger. Winter, who was dressed in a black mohair sweater, black skinny jeans and black fingernails flared up at the mention of a boyfriend and dating.

"Daddy took me to the rodeo. It is his fault! We were in love and daddy ruined it by seeing that woman! She was pathetic. I hate her!" Winter spewed.

"See I thought I saw a picture of you with your arms around a rodeo clown the first time I came to visit. It stuck in my head and I wondered about it. That is why I went in to your room today because I needed to confirm what I remembered" I stated.

I paused to let it all sink in. She put her hands in her face and screamed. I turned toward Mrs. Whitmore. Let us see if I can get her angry enough to spill the beans.

"Mrs. Whitmore, You told me your husband was an award winning rodeo cowboy. Well liked by all. Yet when he had his accident the newspaper interviewed him in the hospital, he blamed his accident on the rodeo clowns. I believe he stated that they were not doing their job and he got thrown around by a bucking bronco injuring his back and ending his career. He sued the rodeo and the rodeo clowns individually. He lost his position on the board because of it; the lawsuit was dropped after his death. He also stated in the article he had death threats starting almost immediately after the law suit" do you care to explain why you withheld that information from me?"

"How did you find that out? The lawsuit was dropped. End of story! What was he supposed to do Esther; he lost his whole world after that accident! I think we have had enough of this, maybe you should leave now"

"One more question, and I will be glad to leave soon. I have a new horse and a family waiting on me to come home. Yet there is still one question no one has answered for me. Did a rodeo clown take advantage of your daughter Winter?"

I looked back and forth between Winter and her mother waiting for a reaction. Winter put her face in her hands and started to cry. Mrs. Whitmore started moving her lips funny like she was biting off some dead skin. They were all on the edge of confession so I needed to land one more arrow to the heart. But first I needed to call Detective Sailor. I excused myself and slipped into the home office to make the call. I just hope he answers.

"Detective, how are you? I miss hearing your voice…I miss you. I know things are sort of ruffled between us right now, and I promise when I get back to the ranch I am going to make it all up to you, but right now I need a favor" I pleaded. Then I began to unfold my theories and suspicions.

Just hearing his voice gave me comfort. Detective Sailor is the constant in my life, my friend first, mentor and yes my love interest. But he was my friend first and always will be. I discussed the case with him at length. Trying to do this on my own was a mistake, I missed details. Two heads are better than one they say; now that phrase really hits home. Law enforcement, criminal investigation units, and even cold case divisions are not made up of a single person and there is a reason for that. Different views, opinions, and ideas are collaborated and needed to solve one case, I need to remember that. We need a crew, a unit, friends, coworkers, or a grouping sometimes and it is okay. I need Detective Sailor in my life in more ways than one, I realize that now.

Feeling good about my talk with the detective, I returned to the Whitmore's. I finished my cup of tea and thanked Summer Whitmore for her hospitality. Then I asked her if she could make some more tea in the kitchen while I talk to her mother and sister a little longer.

Winter Whitmore sat curled up, twirling her dark hair, her black eyeliner running down her face from the tears she shed earlier. She looked lost and scared. Mrs. Whitmore still in her silk gown sat staunchly upright in her cow hide chair. Her perfect nose turned up as if she was that stuck up girl you would pass in the hallway at high school that thought she was better than anyone. Body language tells it all.

"Mrs. Whitmore it has been nearly two years since your husband Anthony was murdered. He was punched in the face and fell to the ground slamming his head on the cement around the pool. Then someone shot him in the stomach. When you shoot someone in the stomach you are either a bad shot, wanted to make a statement, or did not intend to kill, just wound, and send a message. Then however, someone took a very sharp straight edged knife and cut out his tongue. Now that is definitely a message, a message to keep your mouth shut or you talked too much.

"Why are you telling us this, the police told us how he died. He was murdered. I hired you to find out who

did it Miss Valentine! I don't need
details" Mrs. Whitmore stated.

"I am telling you this because it
is obvious to me that more than one
person was there, more than one
person took part in killing your
husband. Possibly three people, but I
suspect just two did the torturing but
one covered it up or turned a blind eye
at least. So you hired me, as you stated
to find out who murdered your
husband. I am explaining who." I
paused to let that sink in a moment.

"I am also explaining what is
going to happen within the next few
hours. Detectives are going to come to
this house and take everyone's
fingerprints. Also they will be searching
the house"

"They searched the house two
years ago! No I will not allow it! It is
time for you to leave Esther Valentine!"

"Oh it is going to happen Mrs.
Whitmore; I just wanted to prepare you.

As a courteous. Then sometime tomorrow I will return so you can pay me the rest of the money for solving the case" I said standing up.

"I...I do not want you to come back. I will get you your dang money now. Just forget it. I cancel my contract with you, so I will pay you to just leave and shut up. I have the money in the office, if you will follow me" She snarled. She glanced over at her daughter Winter. I thought it may be a sign or signal. I held up my hand for her to stop and listen.

"No member of this family will be allowed to leave the house. No going to an auntie's house or a friend's house. Everyone stays put until that doorbell rings!" I said firmly, raising my voice and pointing toward the front door.

Mrs. Whitmore glared at me with those angry eyes that accentuates the phrase...*if eyes could kill.* She turned so swiftly trying to make a statement of disapproval that her gown twirled. She stomped to the office, and returned shortly with an envelope of cash. Then resuming her seat on the cow hide chair, she crossed her legs sharply.

"It is all there, aren't you going to leave now?" Mrs. Whitmore snapped.

I paused and tilted my head listening as the sound of a helicopter filled the room. Winter Whitmore slowly stood up from her folded position on the couch and pointed to the large windows with a view to the back yard.

The Whitmore estate had an acre of freshly mowed lawn behind the house. We gathered at the windows watching as the Bell UH-1 Huey police helicopter landed on the lawn. Soon after, Detective Sailor in his crisp white shirt exited the helicopter along with two other detectives, walked to the house and rang the doorbell...

Chapter 19

Watching Detective Sailor walk across the lawn as he exited the Helicopter was a beautiful sight. I likened it to a scene from a movie where the pilots walk in slow motion across the tarmac. Looking handsome in his white shirt, dark sunglasses the detective strolled across the lawn to the house, made my heart flutter. Instinctively I wanted to run, my hair blowing in the wind, greet him with a kiss, jump into his arms like they do in the movies... but I fought the urge and acted professional in front of everyone. I will get my chance later.

I opened the door to let the detectives in and turned to see all three of the Whitmore women huddled together, holding tightly to one another. Scared, unsure of their future and what was unfolding before them. Detective Sailor gave the other two men that came with him some orders and a list of things to look for. He instructed the family to cooperate and informed them more local police were on the way to assist in the search.

He turned to me and shot me that famous wink of his to let me know we were good. Then took me by the arm as we headed for the door.

"Are you ready for this Esther?" he questioned, one eyebrow raised.

"As ready as I ever will be detective. Do you think our plan will work?" I asked.

"You always have good plans Esther, I trust your instincts" he smiled.

He knew I needed to hear those words. Trust is important in any relationship. We left the Whitmore house and walked to my jeep arm in arm. He opened the car door for me like the gentleman he is and before I got in I turned to face him.

"Thank you for coming detective" I said smiling up at him. "Thank you for trusting me"

Knowing that we were alone, he put his arms around me and pulled me in for one of his giant hugs. I sniffed his neck. The familiar smell of clean soap and chocolate chip cookies drew me in. I relaxed in his arms, pressing my body against his. *This is my happy place* I thought to myself. I never want to let him go.

"Do we have time for a quick bite to eat? Take me to that diner you discovered and I will buy you a large serving of hash browns" he joked.

"Well we will need food detective; it is going to be a long night. And snacks we must have snacks for later. I am thinking gummy bears this time..."

Detective Sailor went to the passenger side of the jeep and got in. We headed straight to the diner in Austin and took a booth in the back.

After ordering we settled in to finishing up the final details of our plan and catching up on the case.

"So I knew it was a two hour drive to Round Rock from Dallas that is when I grabbed the chief and told him what was happening briefly on the case and he told me to take the helicopter"

"You came in big detective. I was impressed. Hearing those blades whirring. It was really something. Watching you step out of that helicopter made my thighs quiver" I giggled.

"Esther I am so happy to be sitting in a diner with you. I missed you. So tell me what is next?"

"We wait till dark detective that is when the magic happens" I teased.

We finished our food still chatting continuously. I introduced him to Kristy the server and she joined us at the booth telling detective Sailor what she had told me about her friend who was involved with the rodeo clown. After she left we talked about Marja, the ranch and our new horse Buddy.

"Buddy is a beautiful horse, Esther. I never know what you are going to bring home after a case, this one surprised me the most. I expect a piece of furniture, a lost sister, but not an animal the size of a small truck"

"Well I just go where life leads me detective. This case led me to rescue Buddy. We have that big chunk of open land just sitting there at the ranch.

Buddy will be happy and live out his life in the open spaces"

"I love your choices Esther, and I love you too"

"I love you detective. I really know that now"

We stayed so long at the diner killing time it was getting dark outside. We slipped into the front seat of the jeep heading for a convenience store for snacks. I could not remember the last time we were this close to each other. It felt good.

Snacks on board we drove to the rodeo and shut off the lights as we rolled in stealthy. Backing the jeep in between the barn and an old white truck. It was white but with one red door. As if the door was transplanted onto this old truck from another old junk discarded truck. We began to wait.

Detective Sailor pulled out the binoculars and quietly got out of the jeep not closing the door all the way. He walked to the edge of the barn crouching, he looked for the site of the bonfire I had told him about where the rodeo clowns sit and drink at night. He pulled up the binoculars to give a quick look then came back and eased back into his seat.

"The fire is barely smoldering and I saw no one sitting there" reported the detective. "We should give it a few more minutes just to be sure"

Concerned the rodeo will close down tomorrow for a break and then start up again in two weeks. We had to do this tonight. It has to work. It is our only hope in solving this case. I popped a few candies in my mouth and offered some to the detective. He scrunched his nose and looked at me like I offered him stinky cheese.

Suddenly we saw beams of light as though someone was walking with a flashlight. We slouched down in the seats till we could barely see over the dash. The flashlight man walked to the office, turned and went back towards the bunk house. Detective Sailor again slipped out of the jeep and went to the edge of the barn but saw no one and came back.

"He must have been patrolling, checking locks. We still need to wait a little while longer if this is going to work Esther"

"It is going to work detective" I said as I reached for his hand. "This is our second stakeout together; how about you pick the snacks next time"

"I think that would be wise considering your choices of chewy snacks, they are sticking to my teeth!"

We held hands and talked quietly letting some time pass. When we both agreed it was the right time we made our move. Slipping out of the jeep we head to the trunk retrieving my rifle, guns, a mega phone, and a long wooden spoon.

"What is the spoon for Esther? Detective Sailor whispered.

"You will see detective. Let's head through the horse barn"

"I will follow you anywhere Esther, I like the view"

"Shhhhsh..." I told him. Even though I was flattered.

We quietly entered the barn at midnight, walked past Buddy's old stall all the way to the end of the horse barn and stopped just before the last stall where a rodeo clown sleeps at night to keep an eye on the horses. I took a fast peek around the corner and I see Baby Boy laying in the hay fast asleep. I held my finger up to my mouth telling detective to remain quiet and we continued on. Exiting the barn at the end gave us direct access to the side of the bunk house that was located behind the second barn. Hoping all the rodeo clowns have gone to sleep for the night.

Detective Sailor positioned himself near the front and only door to the bunk house just to the right. I stayed a little to the left of the door. On the wall of the second barn were nails where the rodeo clowns hung the metal buckets and pails used to feed or groom the horses. I lifted a metal pail from its hook and stood in position. Detective Sailor held his mega phone to his mouth.

We nodded out a count of three and simultaneously I took the wooden spoon banging loudly on the metal pail several times. At the same time Detective Sailor yelled in to the megaphone.

"Fire!! Fire!! Everyone out now!" he yelled. The sound boomed out of the megaphone. He slung it over his shoulder with the strap and took a position with his rifle pointed at the door.

After banging on the metal pail I threw the pail to the ground in front of me then stepped forward and gave the bunkhouse door a few hard bangs. Pulling my revolver, I backed up and took a stance to the right of the bunkhouse door. Detective Sailor gave another command into the megaphone.

Loud panicked voices were heard coming from inside as the rodeo clowns scrambled to get out of what they thought was a burning building. In the distance I could hear sirens as the local police came to join the party.

The first one out was Trip, I recognized him from his muscular arms and tiny waist. I yelled for him to get down on the ground. Next out came Hippie with his bandaged nose. He recognized me, paused, and turned to go back in. Detective Sailor came closer with his rifle pointed at Hippie's face and ordered him to get down on the ground. Tokyo came out of the bunk house door with his hands in the air with a smirk on his face. He noticed the Detective and decided to comply mumbling something under his breath.

Silence. I looked over at Detective Sailor and shook my head letting him know there was still one more. I decided to call him out.

"Ringo, I know you are in there. Might as well come out!"

"Esther, I know that is you. You are one crazy chick. If you want me you will have to come and get me!"

I knew in my gut there was no other way. We had a history. I knew I was going to have to go in. I looked at Detective Sailor and he shook his head no. I worried the choice I was about to make would ruin everything. After we just reconnected, I was about to make the man I love upset by taking chances. I looked at Detective Sailor.

"You have to trust me"

Chapter 20

Reaching down I picked up the metal bucket from the ground I used earlier, and inching closer to the door I tossed it in. There was no reaction from inside. I reached in my cargo pants and pulled out my mag light and held it on top of my revolver. I inched further towards the door and gave one last glance at Detective Sailor. The local police had cleared the area including Baby Boy who had run over from the other barn during the ruckus.

Remembering that Ringo had a knife I proceeded with extreme caution. My police academy training kicked in as I stood at the door, leaned in quickly, and then pulled out trying to see the target. I jumped to the other side of the doorway and shining my flashlight in the room I could see Ringo sitting on a far bottom bunk. He had his hands on his knees staring back at me. He was too calm. He was planning. I nodded at detective Sailor so he would be prepared positioning himself closer to the door. *"We are a team"* I thought to myself. Teams count on each other.

I stepped fully into the room shining my flashlight on Ringo.

"You need to take off your boots slowly and toss them toward me Ringo" I demanded.

"I am not taking off my boots Esther, you can forget that"

"Keep your hands where I can see them at all times Ringo. Where is the knife you keep in your boots?"

"Is that why you want me to take off my boots Esther? I thought you wanted to know my shoe size or something. Dang girl you are a sly one"

"Cut the crap Ringo. My partner and I Detective Sailor want to take you in for questioning, so take off your boots now and get down on the ground. Then put your hands behind your head. Do it now Ringo! This is the last time I am going to tell you!"

"You work for the rodeo just like me Esther. I am not taking off my boots. Now since there is no fire, I think I am going back to sleep" he said nonchalantly laying back on the bunk.

"Listen Ringo, I warned you. Or should I call you Steven? Get down on the ground now!"

That seemed to be the thing that pushed his buttons. He sat up with fire in his eyes. He rose to his feet and took a few steps toward me. I kept my gun aimed at his head. Detective Sailor moved just inside the door aiming the rifle straight at Ringo. The red laser sight began to dance on his forehead. His eyes got bigger realizing this was not a game.

"Who told you my name was Steven? They are a liar who ever they are. Was it Baby Boy? I will slice that short little piece of crap clown!"

"You are not going to slice anyone Ringo. You are going to jail. Turn around and put your hands behind your back now! I am tired of playing this game with you!"

Ringo was looking at the ground briefly. He slowly and methodically raised his head slowly until he locked in on my eyes. He had pure evil in those eyes. I did not move.

"I am the one who is tired of playing this game Esther!" he shrieked.

Simultaneously without losing eye contact Ringo kicked the metal pail I had thrown into the room earlier. Like a football propelling toward the goal post, the metal pail barely missed my head as I quickly tilted to dodge the impact. It bounced off my shoulder and flung toward Detective Sailor, landing at his feet. Ringo lunged at me trying to grab my gun. On impulse, I gave him a swift side kick to the knee and he groaned in pain.

Detective Sailor kept his gun directed at Ringo's head ready to take him out at anytime.

I let go of my gun with my left hand to grab Ringo by the hair to push him to the ground so I could cuff him. His hands reached up to grab me by the waist rendering me helpless for a brief moment as I wrestled to pry his hands loose. My only option was to begin kicking and punching. I landed a solid punch to his right ear, using the butt of the gun to his left, he winced in pain. I saw blood start to trickle. Releasing his grip on my waist, he landed on all fours. Blood dripping on the tile floors. I signaled Detective Sailor and he handed me his handcuffs.

Holstering my weapon I grabbed Ringo by his wrist, snapped on one cuff. As I leaned across him to grab the other wrist, he head butted me, and I taste blood. Angry I stepped back giving him a swift kick to the ribs. He sprawled on the ground moaning. I put a knee in his back and finished cuffing him. Backing up a little dizzy, Detective Sailor stepped forward and caught me. I turned and buried my face in his chest.

"I will get the guys to take him to the station. Suck it up Esther, you did good. It will be alright. We have to maintain our distance remember, unless of course you want to get married, then we can be out in the open with our affection"

I backed up and slapped his chest pushing away. I saw a slight spot of blood from my lip staining his white shirt and started laughing. Trying to keep a straight face I put my hands on my hips and looked him in the eye.

"Detective Sailor, this better not be a proposal because I think I deserve better than you asking me to marry you in a rodeo bunk house with blood on your shirt!" I laughed. I couldn't help it.

He looked down at his shirt and back up at me.

"Now you have to marry me Esther. I got your DNA all over me! Listen before the guys come take this dirt bag away, how did you know his name was Steven?"

"Remember Steven Andrew Miller that purchased the silver Pocket Watch from the Pawn shop? Look at the bottom of Ringo's boots. SAM. Steven Andrew Miller!"

I reached down and pulled off one of Ringo's boots. The knife I saw him with fell out. Turning up the boot and on the bottom it had three initials. SAM. "I bet if we process this knife it will match the same edge that cut the tongue out of Anthony Whitmore"

Ringo hearing our conversation raised his head straining to speak.

"She was cheating on me with that snitch from the rodeo. I went to give her the watch because she told me her dad had one just like it as a gift. She threw it in the dang pool!"

"We better read you your rights Steven Andrew Miller before you say anything else. You will have a chance to tell your whole story to the police" A local Police officer appeared and read him his Miranda rights then took him to be loaded in the police van.

Detective Sailor and I walked toward the jeep, passing the other rodeo clowns being detained. The officer in charge stopped us informing us that Trip, Hippie, and Tokyo all had outstanding warrants. They decided to let Preacher and Baby Boy go as long as we had no objection. We both agreed. They released the cuffs and Baby Boy ran over to me and threw his arms around me.

"Esther, I am so glad you are alright. I was so worried about you dear"

I looked over at detective Sailor and shrugged my shoulders.

"I am just fine Baby Boy. Let me introduce you to my boyfriend and partner Detective Sailor"

"You have a boyfriend? Detective? Are you a cop too Esther?"

"No Manny, however, I was undercover. I hope to see you again someday when we come to the rodeo. Take care of yourself. I have to go to the police station and make a statement now"

As I started to walk away I noticed Detective Sailor had stopped. I looked back to see him shaking hands with Baby Boy then he jogged to catch up with me.

"What was that about?" I asked.

"Oh nothing I was just correcting your mistake"

"What mistake, what did you say to him detective?" I asked stopping to look at him.

"I told him I was not your boyfriend, I was your fiancé and it was so recent that I asked you to marry me that you forgot and gave him the wrong information but he deserved to know the truth" he chuckled and kept walking. I caught up to him.

"Detective Sailor, that was mean. Do I detect a little jealousy? Manny...I mean Baby Boy is harmless. Nothing to worry about there, nope I am all yours"

"Not jealousy sweetheart, I saw the way you watched me today as I was getting out of the helicopter Esther. There was lust in your eyes"

"Oh my, you are on a roll tonight. Are you buying me breakfast?"

We laughed and joked all the way to the jeep. Detective Sailor received a phone call just as we got in the car and turned on the AC. It was from the detectives that were at the Whitmore Estate. As he hung up he turned to give me the details.

"Well Esther your hunch was right again. The only print that was lifted from the murder scene that was unaccounted for was Winter Whitmore. His own daughter"

"That is sad Detective. Apparently she was in a relationship with Ringo, or Steven Andrew Miller I guess, but after he already had a fight with Connie his ex-girlfriend. Ringo dated Winter just to aggravate her father and get information I am sure. Romancing Winter, Steven found out that Anthony Whitmore was the new man in Connie's life and that he had purchased her a home. He remembered Anthony Whitmore as the man who blamed the rodeo clowns for his accident. When Mr. Whitmore found out his daughter was dating a rodeo clown he forbid her to see him"

"Another child thinking if daddy was dead, I can do what I want and run off with the man of my dreams scenario, huh Esther"

"Yes detective. It was all a plan. Sadly Ringo never had any real feelings for Winter. He used her. This all snowballed in to a murder plot to kill Anthony Whitmore. I believe you will find out that Winter shot her father but not being a sharp shooter she aimed for his stomach. Ringo had already punched him in the face so when Winter botched up the shooting, Ringo decided to send a message as well as finish the job to end Mr. Whitmore's life. He ignorantly thought he could get Connie Munro back with Mr. Whitmore out of the way"

"That message being that you don't blame the rodeo clowns for your accidently falling from a bucking bronco?"

"Exactly, it almost put the rodeo out of business when he filed the lawsuit. Ringo would have lost his job and the girl. It was too much for him, and he snapped. I figured it all out when I remembered that Baby Boy was drunk one night, telling me that Ringo's name must be Sam because it is written on the bottom of his boots"

"You are brilliant Esther, and I am pretty special too"

"Oh really how did you come to that conclusion detective?"

"I let you handle that rodeo clown all by yourself. You were amazing, except for the bloody lip"

Chapter 21

As usual we had to stop at the local precinct and fill them in on the whole story. I turned in the picture of Winter Whitmore arm in arm with Ringo, the silver pocket watch and gave my statement for the time I worked at the rodeo. Detective Sailor filled in the rest and notified the cold case unit. I knew the news media would be chomping to get the story. The Whitmore murder was all over the news when it happened.

Detective Sailor was still talking as I slipped in to a nearby office and got comfortable on the couch. I routinely stay away from the crowds. Police precincts have the best couches if you ever need to close your eyes a bit.

It was nearly dawn when Detective Sailor woke me up stating we can go home, so I sat up and patted the couch for him to join me. Wiping the sleep out of my eyes then checking my breath by blowing in my hand, I leaned in for a kiss.

"If you take me home detective, I will love you forever"

"I will love you forever too Esther but hasn't anyone ever told you that the blowing in your hand to check your breath does not actually work? We need a breath mint. Let's go get that breakfast and go home to the ranch"

I was mortified. I checked my breath again and looked up at him.

"It works doesn't it?"

"No Esther it does not, it smells like you have been eating sardines. Can we go now, I am starving"

"If you are this grumpy in the morning I do not know if I will marry you after all Detective Sailor!"

"I am kidding Esther" he said whispering. "Really I just want to get out of here so I can kiss you back; there are too many eyes on us right now" he said glancing around.

He took me by the hand and led me out of the police station. When we reached the jeep he stopped. Leaned me up against the door and kissed me so hard I thought I would faint. I love this man completely. We make a good team.

We had a two hour drive ahead of us so we decided to stop at a diner and get some coffee and food in us. Ham, eggs and hash browns always taste better when you have been up all night. I called Marja to tell her it was over and I was coming home to the ranch. She did her usual squeal with delight.

"Esther, that is great. Does this mean no more clowns?" she asked.

"No more clowns in my life for a long while Marja. How is Buddy liking the ranch?"

"Wait till you see him Esther. He ran the length of the fence, twice! He is very happy in his new home. Can you bring home some hay?"

"I will see what I can do. There is a Livestock feed supply not too far from the ranch. Did mother make it in with her RV yet?"

"Yes, that is why I am up so early. She arrived at 6am. Gave me a scare hearing the door open. We need an alarm system for the ranch, hurry home Esther"

Settling in for the drive back, holding hands with Detective Sailor as he drove my jeep, I feel accomplished like all is right in the world. Bad guys are in jail, no injuries except a busted lip that still smarts a little. Heading home to my ranch just in time for winter to really begin and looking forward to the holidays with my family. However, a case stays with you forever. Always wondering if I could have done something different. Happy that you solved a case and gave family members closure they needed but at the same time I know they will have a hard time healing form the pain and anguish they have just gone through.

"I can't help but feel sorry for Mrs. Whitmore. She lost her husband to murder and then she finds out her daughter Winter Whitmore is the one that shot him. How does a family heal from that sort of trauma detective?"

"I cannot say they heal Esther, I think they just learn to cope day to day"

"What will happen to Winter?"

"I am sure Winter will do some time in jail, the bullet wound she inflicted on her father was not fatal, but still she was accessory to murder. She watched it happen. It was the cutting out of the tongue by Steven Andrew Miller that did him in. Ringo will most likely do life behind bars"

"Ringo behind bars gives me comfort. He was the meanest Rodeo clown and very angry. He did try to challenge me and I thought we were going to fight several times. I came close to facing down the same knife that cut out Mr. Whitmore's tongue"

"You just need some time to relax before the next cold case Esther. I did hear a rumor from Marja that you broke someone's nose, is this true?"

"Yes it is true. I cracked his rib as well. It was the rodeo clown they called Hippie. I half expected he would be wearing tye dye but he did wear a pink cowboy hat. Yep he wanted me to leave the rodeo and when I didn't he reared his arm back to take a swing, but I blocked him and busted his nose"

"I wish I would have seen you ride Buddy the horse. Maybe another time. Excluding the rodeo clowns of course"

"You will just have to settle watching me ride Buddy the horse on the ranch detective"

We arrived in Dallas and we had to drop Detective Sailor off at his car, the baby blue cougar. Seeing as he took the police helicopter to assist me in Round Rock.

"My plans are to say hello to everyone at the ranch then crash for a few hours detective, but I would love it if you come to the ranch for dinner. I am sure with mother and Marja there it will be something tasty and interesting"

"Yum, your mother's frozen pizza and Marja's famous burritos. Sounds good I will be there. I have to check in at the station, run a few errands, and then crash myself. See you about seven-ish?"

A quick hug and kiss good-bye and I headed the jeep toward the ranch, just south of Dallas. It was turning cloudy, windy, and cold. I think it will be a record cold winter this year. Possibly snow. I would love a white Christmas. Marja has never seen snow.

I pull into the small feed store nearest to the ranch and purchase a bale of hay, some sweat feed and a horse blanket to keep Buddy warm in the cold. We have an old barn on the ranch we can open up and put it to good use if Marja has not already thought about it. That girl is always one step ahead of me. As the employee helps me load the hay in the jeep I cringed. The two Stetson hats I purchased from Whitmore Western Wear are still in the back of the jeep. I do not like the thought of hay in my new jeep so I went back inside and made arrangements for hay delivery every month. Errands done.

I pull into the gate at the ranch and honk my horn as I drive down the long dirt road to the house like I usually do. There was a time I was the only one here and had no one to come home to. Things have surely changed for the better with Marja around.

I can see Mother's RV parked to the side of the house and I have to chuckle. I hope I am as active and brave as she is when I am her age. Marja came out to greet me as I parked next to the old jeep I handed down to little sis.

"I am so glad you are home Esther. Buddy will be so glad to see you. I opened up that old barn they used to put cattle in when this was a working ranch. I hope you don't mind, but with winter cold coming Buddy needs a warm barn"

"I can always count on you Marja. I am so glad to be home. I brought you a gift"

"I love gifts Esther, but it can wait until after dinner. You go get some sleep. Detective Sailor will be here about seven"

"You talked to Detective Sailor?"

"Umm yes but I wasn't supposed to tell you. He wants me to help him plan a little surprise for you. You didn't hear that! Go rest now Esther"

I found mother in the kitchen and we hugged. She was glad to see me as much as I was to see her. We promised to sit and catch up later so I headed upstairs. I fell asleep instantly. There is nothing like being in your own bed, at home, with no clowns.

Marja woke me at six pm and I headed to the shower to be ready for dinner and the arrival of Detective Sailor. When I emerged from the bathroom Marja was there laying clothes on the bed for me to wear.

"Marja, I am not feeling fancy tonight. I want to throw on sweat pants and put my hair in a pony tail"

"No Esther you must look pretty for Detective Sailor. Do not argue. He is waiting for you down stairs"

I was shocked that he had already arrived knowing how exhausted we were. He must be looking forward to dinner. I know I am starving and looking forward to Marja's cooking as well. I put on the black slacks Marja laid out for me and a white long sleeve sweater. Combed my hair, applied the usual cherry pink lip gloss, and went down stairs.

As I walked into the large living room with the stone fireplace I could smell the wood burning. The smells of winter and the holidays includes a wood burning fireplace. Detective Sailor is standing in front of the stone fireplace with one hand behind his back and the other in his pocket. He looked handsome as ever.

Mother was sitting on one couch and Marja was sitting across from her on the other couch. Their eyes lit up as I walked in the room as if they were up to something. Boldly I walked right up to Detective Sailor and gave him a kiss. Might as well, it is our thing and our relationship is no longer a secret to Marja and my mother.

I stood back admiring his beautiful face. Suddenly he brought out a beautiful bouquet of star gazer lilies from behind his back and gave them to me. My favorite flowers are star gazer lilies. They smell like Noxzema.

"How did you know these were my favorite flower detective? They are absolutely beautiful. I love them, thank you. This is such a sweet surprise!"

"Marja helped me a little. I have one more surprise for you Esther"

"Oh I also have a surprise for you as well should I go get it?"

Detective Sailor grabbed my hand and looked me in the eyes. I decided the Stetson hat could wait a while, maybe after dinner. I saw so much love in his sparkling eyes I could not look away.

All of a sudden Detective Sailor knelt down on one knee still holding my hand. My heart starting beating faster. He reached in his pocket and pulled out a little black box. He opened it and held it up to face me.

"Esther Valentine, I have loved you since the day I met you when you were just seventeen. I will love you forever and always. I love how you always bring home something from each case you solve. I embrace your family, your work, the furniture free ranch, and your strong stubborn spirit.

Esther, will you marry me?"

About the Author

Rebecca is a writer of Historical Fiction. She retired from Hospital work after 27 years, and now lives with her husband in Florida. She loves including historical facts, cities, and sites in her books alongside fictional Characters. She also loves writing strong female heroines in her books as well.

Her three grown children and grandchildren keep her busy, but never too busy to write full time. Her latest series - *Esther Valentine Chronicles*: a crime series has four books already in the series and another on the way.

Rebecca and her husband John, enjoy traveling. They have traveled Europe and around the USA in an RV for two years and loved it. Rebecca enjoys writing and including stories about the places she has visited in her books.

Book Four –<u>Silver Pocket Watch</u>. Esther solves a murder case gone cold in Austin, Texas.

Book Five – To be announced...

Look for more books in the Esther Valentine Chronicles coming soon....

Follow Me

Facebook: Facebook.com/Irishbonesbook1

Twitter: @Rebecca29971384

Webpage: http://rebalexa.wixsite.com

Instagram: Rebecca.a.bruce

Goodreads:
https://www.goodreads.com/author/show/205
93959.Rebecca_Conaty_Bruce

Allauthor:
https://allauthor.com/author/rebb/

Amazon Author page links:
amazon.com/author/rebeccaconatybruce
https://amzn.to/30YmdED

End Notes:

Although this story is fictional some of the procedures mentioned are real and can be harmful if not done properly and with consent. No rodeo clowns were harmed in the writing of this book.

- ✓ Honor your parents; they know what is best for you!

- ✓ Never put you or anyone you love in danger. Keep guns safely locked up and away from children.

- ✓ If you find yourself in an abusive relationship please reach out and ask for help.

To my devoted followers:

I hope you enjoy following Esther Valentine and her crime solving techniques. Thanks for reading Shades of Murder: The Esther Valentine Chronicles, Sincerely,

Rebecca Conaty Bruce

D.T. - Amazon reviewer wrote:

"This book was well written and easy to read. It held my interest the whole way through. I look forward to reading more books written by this author!"

allauthor.com wrote:

An entertaining, wholesome, and enjoyable mystery with well-drawn characters.

A well-written story with a wonderfully endearing cast of characters. Really love this series